THE GIRL WITH THE
THOUSAND-YARD STARE

The Girl with the Thousand-Yard Stare

—

Stuart Maskell

ISBN: 1507788274
ISBN 13: 9781507788271
Library of Congress Control Number: 2015902028
CreateSpace Independent Publication Platform
North Charleston, South Carolina

For my wife and my wonderful Mother and Father who I will never be able to thank enough.

The following took place in England over the past few decades.

The names have been changed to protect the innocent.

TABLE OF

CONTENTS

CHAPTER 1

JAMES.

———

B Y THE TIME YOU READ this I will be dead.
My name is James Thomas Forester.

Believe it or not I waited years for the right person to come along and then I entrusted my story to a man I met in the pub!

So here goes.

When I was a little boy I was, shall we just say, "interfered with" by the local Catholic Priest. Now the fact that he was Catholic has nothing to do with it, he was a paedophile, Period.

The point is I took this secret to my grave, I kept it all my life only realizing toward the end how much it impacted on me, my relationships and the things that I did.

Anyway this is not all about me and it's certainly not about the Catholic church, it's about the people I held dear, their lives and the hope that even though unspeakably bad things happen, good people always win.

Toward the end of our time on this earth we all have to make choices. I chose family, new unlikely friendships and the cherry on the top, a nice big helping of retribution!

CHAPTER 2

HOW IT ALL BEGAN

———

Peter. Winter. 2005.

S O I WAS HAVING A couple of beers as blokes like me do whenever the chance presents itself. It was Christmas 2005, I think, and I was in an old village inn, which is a "pub" or a "bar" to you and me. The huge metal sign swinging in the wind outside said this in big letters: The Carpenters Arms. And under that, much smaller, it read: warm beer and cold food.

Now I am sure one of the reasons I chose this pub was because of its obvious sense of humor.

It was a classic British country pub like you would see on a postcard of a quintessential English village or in a movie starring Jude Law and Kate Winslet. It had a thatched roof, low ceilings, oak beams, real ale, an open fire, a wet sleeping dog in the corner, and pies and chips. It was that sort of place.

My name is Peter Carrington, and I had only been in England for a few days, having returned for the holidays to visit the folks, deliver presents, eat too much, argue with my dad, and play charades. Then I would fly back to New York. I was missing the wife and kids, who couldn't come that year, and so therefore I went to the pub.

I had moved to the United States about twenty-two years before, so as you can imagine, flying home for Christmas had become quite a regular thing. Mum appreciated it, and I sort of enjoyed seeing the family and some old friends. After all, it's only once a year, so I grinned and bore it.

Mum and Dad had moved to the country when Dad had retired from the army some years ago. It had been a much-needed break from the fast pace of London. This place couldn't have been accused of being fast at anything. There were just a few walkers, some students, and some golfers.

The pub was advertising an open mic night that would take place on the next Sunday. The words were highlighted on a chalkboard as if the event was not to be missed at any cost. We were not completely out in the sticks by any stretch of the imagination, but we were far enough from the nearest city, so our little town was virtually tourist-free at this time of the year. In the summer there was the riverboat traffic, and being reasonably close to London, you always get visitors, but not like they do in say Windsor or Bath.

It was about five o'clock in the afternoon when I first met James, but I didn't get to know him until after dinner when I made my excuses and returned to the bar. I had no idea at the time that this intriguing Englishman would soon change my life immeasurably. But I will get to that.

Mum and Dad were meeting me in the pub at seven thirty for dinner, and I had a combination of jet lag and a taste for the local ale, so I was firmly planted on a very comfortable barstool by four o'clock in the afternoon.

The weather outside had turned dramatic even for the United Kingdom at that time of the year, so I didn't feel too guilty about being in a warm, dry pub so early in the day. It was already becoming dark outside, and another long winter night was starting.

It was the sort of place where if you sat on a sofa, people assumed you needed to be left alone. But on the other hand, if you sat at the bar, it was clear that you wanted to talk to the other patrons or to the staff. I think the bar staff there had been trained in the art of small talk for that exact reason—or maybe they were naturals.

So I safely assumed that the other people at the barstools were much the same as me and wanted to pass the time of day. If not they would have moved to a sofa or pretended to read the paper. So I started by chatting with the bar staff. There was the usual clash of horns between old has-beens like me and the part-time lifeguard, part-time barman, part-time doorman Hugh Grant look-alike on the other side of the slab of elm. I looked like even more of an old has-been to the drop-dead gorgeous, brain-dead barmaid.

Both the barmaid and the barman said the same things. It was all pretty standard stuff. They'd ask questions like, "Where are you from?" or "What brings you here?" And after they didn't listen to my answers, they'd respond, "Oh, really. That sounds interesting. You must know my dad." Then I'd feel old and I'd fail at telling a joke. You get the picture.

He sat next to me, didn't get involved, and just looked at his beer, but I saw him glance my way from time to time, especially when I tried the same joke on a different barmaid or when I went a little too far with the wisecracks. So I knew he was taking it all in and that a conversation would be easy to initiate.

By then, he knew that I was from the United States but that I used to live in England, that I was married with kids, that I was forty-four, and that I was an attorney in New York.

He must have heard me tell someone that my name was Peter and certainly must have overheard me tell the inquiring barmaid about my wife, Sandi, and about how she was a journalist for the *New York Times*, and he may have listened when I gushed about my two young girls.

I guess he noted, as did everyone else in there, that I can be a stereotypical loud American but that I am also a good listener. After all, I had endured a half hour of the slip-of-a-thing barmaid pouring her heart out about her dramatic and life-changing breakup from her boyfriend of three weeks.

He was a little odd looking. He didn't stand out from the crowd, but the way he held himself implied something out of the ordinary. He was the sort of guy I usually stayed clear of, not because he looked like trouble, but because he looked a bit, well, boring. Little did I know that I was about to spend the next four nights sitting there and listening to him talk.

He was in his mid-fifties, I would say, but he didn't look at all well, and something heavy hung on his shoulders. He had graying but thick and distinguished-looking hair that was cut regularly, but he wasn't the type to put products in it. He wore the sort of clothes that say, "I don't care much about my appearance, but I am smart, clean, and orderly." They were neither branded nor trendy nor old nor tatty. Come to think of it, he had probably chosen to look exactly like that at some point, and it had stuck. It said something about him and allowed him to be invisible but imposing at the same time or maybe at the flick of a switch. Picture a cross between your old chemistry teacher and Richard

Gere. I guessed that he had a wardrobe of that stuff and dressed much the same each day. His clothes were almost a uniform with tweed and brogues and checked shirts.

So I said, "Hi, I'm Peter. What's up, buddy?"

He said hello back and then preceded to grill me about my life and loves. About why anyone would ever leave this glorious country for a godforsaken land such as America. He had a point. But I defended the good old US of A as you would and bit by bit filled him in on at least the latter part of my uneventful life.

You see when it comes right down to it, I had to explain to him that I am a plain and simple man. The only exciting thing I ever did was to have a huge fight with my folks and run off to college in America. The fact that we made up straight after and have been close ever since is largely irrelevant and being separated by a vast stretch of cold water probably made it easier to miss one another. What we actually fell out about was so silly now and yet it was so serious at the time. Dad wanted me to be a doctor, but Mum wanted me to stick to my lifelong plan to be a vet. It's true I had declared my intention to work with animals since before I could walk, but I was a grown man now and I was going to do what I wanted, not what they told me to do. So I deliberately decided to study law just to piss them off. As was my intention it pissed them off. They were sure I was making a mistake, and the more they tried, the more I dug in. One thing led to another and in a blink of an eye I was in America feeling like the big man even though my mum had paid for the airfare.

Once I found myself over there and alone, I just got by on my looks, I told James and that made everyone in the pub laugh. In reality I wasn't alone for long by pure luck. I quite literally bumped into Sandi, my now wife, as we ran in opposite directions through the park one evening. That sort of thing happens all the time and people tend to just pick themselves up, apologize, dust themselves off, mutter something under their breath about watching where the hell they are going next time, and move on. Unfortunately, or fortunately as it matrimonially turned out, we couldn't do that because we were both unconscious! She for a few seconds longer than I, but both of us were out cold for a short while. Long enough for people to gather and for someone to call an ambulance which we shared and in which we just held our own heads in our hands, and then as we looked up at each other, we just burst out laughing. It turned out no lasting damage had been done, mild concussion and a big matching lump on each of our foreheads but nothing serious. We rode the subway together and then went our separate ways only exchanging phone numbers out of human kindness. She probably never expected to see me again. I had other ideas and called her as soon as I got to my apartment.

At first she played hard to get; Sandi says it's because she genuinely didn't like me very much, but I would rather think it's just what good girls do. Either way I eventually ground her down and we started going out about a year after our stars collided!

Sandi is, of course, never wrong. Women never are or so they constantly tell me, but when she said that she had decided to be a journalist and that it wasn't some sort of last resort, I thought she had gone mad. I am sure it's a great fun job and that you expect to get to travel the world, but she was bright at college and I always had her down as a city girl, you know, Wall Street sort of stuff. She is great with math and languages and that sort of academic stuff, and journalists get paid squat, right? Well, she does get paid squat, but I think in the long run she was right all along. Being a freelance journalist means flexibility without which we may not have been able to marry and have kids so young. She's happy. We are happy. And that's kind of what counts in the end I think.

I, on the other hand, had chosen a career just to piss my Dad off and now I hated my job and I was stuck with it for life, because I was good at it and it paid well and we have a huge mortgage and kids' school fees and I refuse to fly coach long haul because of my long legs but moreover my general aversion to having contact with the great unwashed.

So obviously I had divulged most of the above to James that night in some small detail, and I recall he listened and was inquisitive, and I liked that for a rare occasion I was coming over as quite an interesting person even though I didn't personally believe that I was for a second. I still have no idea why I chose that night to be so open to a stranger and God only knows why James chose that same night to tell me his staggering story, but that's what happened. Perhaps we saw things in each other that reminded us of ourselves or the person we wanted to be? Or more accurately the person we should be if we just shook off our overtly normal persona for once? Perhaps the time was just right?

I do remember how James paid particular attention when I talked about my two children, Fay and Jaz. His mood changed when I said how proud I was of them both getting into good schools and onto one sports team or another, and as every parent does I probably oversold them quite a bit. I mean kids are hard work, right? And they drive you mad. My two are no exception, but when you talk about them to strangers in a bar, you describe them as if they were little angels. No one says that their teenage daughters are moody hormonal bitches that deliberately bring home boys they know their dad will hate, do they?

After dinner he was still there at the same spot, so I sat back down at the bar and we continued where we left off. We seemed to know each other a little by then or maybe it was because I'd had too many glasses of good red wine, but whatever it was that gave me the nerve to pry, I asked James about the elephant in the room. I went and asked him about his obvious ill health.

He took a moment. From the way he cleaned his upper teeth with his tongue, I knew he was deciding whether or not to spill something really juicy. Despite the long awkward silence, I suspected that there was an answer on the way. From the way he carefully set down his pint and then slowly turned to look right at me, I got the impression that what he was about to say was not going to be a simple one-word reply about his general well-being. Instead, and bear in mind the fact that we had really only just met, he led me, slowly at first, into what turned out to be the most incredible story I'd ever heard and one which I ended up being a part of.

CHAPTER 3

WHO NEEDS
A DRINK?

———

James and Peter. Winter. 2005.

"IT'S LIKE THIS," JAMES SAID. "When a man gets to a certain age, he looks in the mirror and wonders what it's all about. How did I go from a spotty teenager with all the worries in the world to this? I mean, I'm a genuinely certified old man with real and actual worries. Like a mortgage that I thought I would have paid off years ago. Credit and store cards from shops I have never heard of. A dog that hates me, and a cat I hate that we inherited when our neighbors moved back to Brazil without so much as a by-your-leave.

"I mean, seriously, how do we end up like this? Who needs a camping trailer or three life jackets or antique-looking golf clubs? Why do I still have brightly colored plastic sleds and roller skates? When did the car stop going in the garage, and when did the garage start bursting with bikes, go-carts, and wet suits that no longer fit anyone?

"I just don't know how it happens. I totally get that it does just happen and that everyone looks in the mirror and thinks that they are starting to look like their dad or mum or whatever. But with me, it was more than that. It was just as if I had never grown up—never changed at all really on the inside. But to look at me, you would think I had become a completely different person.

"I always wondered whether it was just me, and I suspected it was not. Probably we all can't believe how time has flown by. I just don't understand how I could still feel so underdeveloped. So unchanged or ungrown and like I didn't do whatever I was supposed to do between the ages of seventeen and fifty.

"After all, I've got a good family name—or so they tell me—and I've known success in parts. For example, take my marriage to Laura, who has always been out of my league. Or take my beautiful son, Jake, who gets his great looks from his mum. I think he's happy and already doing better than I am in every way possible. And there's my job at the university, which I actually love and which thankfully pays well enough. And I'm an OK bloke, or so I've been told.

"I have friends, and I used to be in a band. I did well in school and wasn't beaten up every day. But still, I have this sense of underachievement and discontent and a distinct impression that after I die no one will give a rat's ass. So I decided to do something about it. I can't actually remember deciding—I just did. It was probably on one of those mornings when the mirror looked disapprovingly back at me as I shaved. It didn't just happen to me. I made it happen, and I don't regret a single thing."

"I can't believe I am saying this stuff out loud, let alone to someone I just met, but it seems easier than with friends or family. It's probably the beer talking, but it feels good. I've got issues, Peter. Big issues. If you will bear with me for a bit and let me rant away, I promise I have quite a story to tell you in the end."

I said that I didn't mind at all. In fact it was great to just sit and listen to someone else rant on endlessly for a change. Being an attorney I am usually the one making the long speeches.

So James continued, "This is going to sound out there, but I have had or rather I have got cancer. There I said it. This feels good!"

I said I was sad to hear that and when did he first find out. I wasn't expecting quite as much detail.

"It was about this time last year," James said, "and I was in the shower...I know it's gross and nasty to talk about. I was washing, and it was like, 'Wait a minute—that's not right. That's new!' And then I panicked and I shouted for Laura and ran down the stairs, and oh my God!

"I know, it's all embarrassing stuff, but blokes don't tend to spend too much time checking our nuts, which I know we should, but that's men for you. And I never thought I was a bloke in the way people who go to football matches on coaches with other strange men are definitely blokes. But it turns out I am one, because I didn't check my nuts regularly for lumps. But there it was—a lump. A big lump.

"'I don't think it was there a month ago,' I said to Laura as if that was when I had last checked myself, which it certainly wasn't.

"Laura got on her hands and knees, and I suddenly jumped back, hit the wardrobe door and cut the back of my bare leg. After I calmed down, I locked the bathroom door and turned on as many bright lights as I could. She crouched down again as I looked up at the ceiling and very nearly whistled. She helped by rolling and squeezing and rolling. And then she let go, thank God. Then she sat on the loo and just looked up at me with her hands on her knees. I knew then that it was bad. I knew then that our plans for the future together had just changed.

"So I went to see the doc as soon as I could. First, though, it was the usual, 'Press this for that and that for this,' and 'Your call is important to us.' The receptionist asked me why I needed an appointment so urgently. And did it have to be 'my' doctor? I just lost it and told her that I had a gigantic hairy lump on my privates, and she put me straight through. But anyway, after a load of hassle, I got an appointment and in I went. Now this is when it gets gross!

"It was bad enough having a feel of my own junk in the shower. It was even worse calling in my wife to come take a closer look. But to have a strange man fiddling about with my—well, that was just not the best day of my life.

"I was more apprehensive about dropping my pants in front of the doctor than I was about what he might say about the lump. I had avoided the dreaded prostate check for years. In fact, I had never been back to see him since he had suggested that it was getting 'about that time' nine years before. I had gotten away with not having my prostate checked now for sure because there were clearly bigger fish to fry, so to speak.

"I did as he asked and sat on the bed, lay back, and took down my pants. I sat there just mortified and asked him if he was sure the door was locked. He didn't reply.

"He was by then engrossed in my testicles, and he had a less than encouraging look on his face. My apprehension had gone with my dignity. I began by asking what he thought my chances were, but after no reply, I said something like, 'What ya think, Doc?' which came out in a strange accent for some reason. He either didn't hear me or was ignoring me thankfully. He just continued to examine me and to scrunch up his eyes and nose. Then he slowly stepped away from my undercarriage, took off his gloves, discarded them in the waste bin without taking his eyes off of my nether region, and leaned back on the edge of his oak desk.

"I was sitting there. I didn't even think to pull up my pants—I just sat there. He leaned back, and if his hands hadn't just been where they had been, I think he would have had one hand on his chin as he told me that he thought it was possibly quite serious and that he was referring me immediately to an oncologist who will have a closer look and probably perform a biopsy.

"I dressed as he talked about options, outcomes, statistics, early detection, and oncologists' tests to determine this and that. And then just like that, we were looking at each other, and he didn't know what to say. He clearly thought I had something really bad. It was written all over his face, and I was the one who felt sorry for him, not the other way 'round because I was making him feel bad. I felt I should leave as quickly as possible, and so I did.

"I had to somehow convince myself it wasn't cancer. It could be a cyst, I thought, or even if it was cancer, at least it was in the testicle which anyone can do without, can't they? I read none of the literature that the doctor gave me either. I think it's still in the glove box of the car to this day.

"That night, I told Laura the doctor wasn't at all worried about it. That simple lie to Laura meant that I then had to perpetuate the story at least until after the oncologist had seen me. Maybe even until after the results of those tests, or maybe even after that. So I did. And it helped. I was living the lie, and it helped—for a few weeks, anyway.

"So only a few days later I was in to see the oncologist for the expected biopsy. He turned out to be a very old friend of mine called Dr. David Houser. We went to school together and then even the same university. Perhaps that's how come I didn't have to wait very long for an appointment?

"He had the pleasure of coming face to face with my undercarriage, which by now I was getting used to people doing. The biopsy was done with quite a painful needle, and then the terrible waiting game commenced."

By that time on that first memorable evening, it was getting late. After his initial monologue, the conversation drifted off in the usual directions—pub talk about what we had done, places we had visited, and other normal topics. I told him about the time I tried to run the New York City Marathon, and he didn't seem unimpressed. He trumped that, and on we went into the witching hour and beyond.

Then I woke up with an unavoidable hangover and had a day from hell with Mum, Dad, their friends, and their friends' kids. We had some leftover turkey that was by then two days too dry. There was much small talk, and I think we even played a game of Trivial Pursuit.

My mum loves Christmas and all that it entails, and she is a fabulous cook, which made up for the headache a little. Then as the day wore inexorably on, the conversation from the night before began to come back to me. The more it did, the more I planned to go back to the pub that night.

I had no idea if he would be there again or if the storytelling would continue, but I made my lame excuses, and straight after dinner at about eight, I slipped out into the wintery night air on the off chance that it would. Mum was fine about it, and Dad was asleep, so off I went in the rain to see if I could find my way back to the same barstool. I had only been in the pub for enough time to have about half a beer when the barstool next to him became available. Although now I think I should have played it a bit cooler, I jumped on it in a childishly too-obvious way. He smiled a knowing but friendly smile that I took to mean I was welcome, and so very soon after pleasantries, we were back to trading rounds of cold beer for stories. Thankfully, it soon became a one-sided conversation.

CHAPTER 4

BAD NEWS
TRAVELLING FAST

———

James. Winter. 2004.

JAMES CONTINUED, "I WAS BACK at the oncologists for the dreaded results a very long ten days later and sitting in the waiting room pretending to read a virus-covered old copy of *Hello* magazine, which I know for a fact thirty people had sneezed over. I think I had it open to the same page for twenty minutes, and I vaguely remember that it was open at an article about someone from a boy band called 'Take That' and his fabulous wedding.

"Anyway, God knows what people thought, as I couldn't care less about Garry Whoever and his silk-lined frock coat. So I'm sitting there in a daze when I hear, 'James Forester, James Forester.' The announcement came over the loudspeaker, you see. And I think they had been calling me for ages. I already knew what the doctor was going to say, and I had somehow started to dissolve into the chair.

"I don't recall what I was thinking about, but it was already bad thoughts—end thoughts like plans I'd made, dreams I'd had, stuff I should have done, and stuff I needed to get done before…well, you know. And anyway, there was the loudspeaker again, and this time someone with a mild cold who shouldn't have even been there—one of my students from college, I think—prodded me, and I was up and gone in a flash. Like someone woken from a deep sleep to find he had left the bath running.

"He's a nice enough chap, Dr. Houser. I went to Plymouth University with him, where I did economics and David did medicine. Actually, the only reason we went was because it wasn't home and it was the closest university to the surfing beaches of Devon and Cornwall.

"So I don't think I ever thought of him as my doctor in the way other people think of theirs because I remembered him from college. He drank, smoked pot, and hung around with girls—the usual childish pranks and mischief.

"We were kids even at college, and I still think of him on his motocross bike, and not as a very capable senior doctor.

"He, I am sure, sees me on my skateboard with that questionable haircut I had for far too long. He doesn't, I am sure, see me as a semi-capable economics professor who turned down an offer for a job with share options at Goldman Sachs just before they took over the world of finance. Not at all bitter!

"But sure as night follows day, there we both were in his drab consultation room with its obligatory poster of the insides of a human next to pictures of his kids and certificates in frames that were clearly meant to put one at ease.

"I always wonder about those certificates on people's office walls and whether I could get away with putting my swimming certificate up in my study instead of my actual qualifications. I think I could.

"I bet that while David was thinking of the best way to break it to me, he remembered the time I caught him and Sue Millard in a compromising position. It was bad enough that they were in my mum's bathroom, but at the time, Sue was going out with a close friend of mine, and David and I had just met. In fact, that was our very first meeting!"

"Maybe he had a more pleasant flashback to the time we went to France in his dad's camper van long before either of us was competent at driving on this side of the road, let alone in France in a huge camper van.

"Anyway, as doctors sometimes do, he was finishing up something from his previous patients' notes as

I came in and without looking up he said, 'Take a seat,' but I already had.

"I won't bore you with all of the details, but after the embarrassing bit and a long awkward pause, he delivered it straight. And then, just like that, I was gone and I was in the car and driving with people's faces and the rain passing by. My windshield wipers were on and all too often so were my brake lights. I was late for work for the second time in my adult life, the first being when Laura gave birth to the twins twenty-five years ago.

"David's surgery is quite close to my house, so it can be an hour from there to work. Being late was on my mind more than it should have been given the fact that I had just been told I was on my last legs. See, I had been listening. Cancer is a bitch, that's for sure.

"I know now that I should have gone the other way—gone home to Laura—but I was on autopilot. I had gotten up that morning in the usual way. Showered and dressed in the usual way. Set off for work at the usual time. Only that day, I was going to the doctor's en route. I clearly hadn't thought it through, but work was where I was going, no matter what.

"I thought about the time that Laura and I said we would buy an abandoned old farmhouse in France when we could afford it, but Jake then grew up so fast, life happened, and the moment was gone.

"I started to fall into the obvious spiral of regrets and 'what ifs,' 'should haves,' and 'if onlys.' You can imagine the stuff—it's all been said and done a thousand times, and I suppose most of us will sadly have that internal monologue near the end.

"Anyway, when it happens to you, leave it alone—trust me. It's of no use. What's done is done, and what you should be doing with the little time you have left is digging out the life insurance details, sorting your will, selling the classic car collection (if only you had one), and spending the proceeds on a family holiday.

"What you should do as soon as you leave the doctor's car park is get your house in order. After that, if there's time, be nice to your wife and kids like never before, and try to have some fun. Only once everything else is done should you take a moment to look down at the tea-stained mug and feel sorry for yourself or angry at God or the asbestos firm or whoever you can blame.

"Better still would be to look up at the stars and smile and say something from a movie, something profound like, 'It's been a wonderful ride, really.' Because it probably has been.

"And when you're told that you're on your way out at just fifty-one years old, the last thing you should ever do—and trust me, I can vouch for this as the absolute last thing anyone should do—is drift off into a self-pitying stupor. For months! Literally months!"

CHAPTER 5

A MUCH-
NEEDED LIFT

—

James. January 2004.

"LISTEN, PETER," JAMES SAID, "I am not a very spiritual man and I think you have probably gathered by now that I am not a complete nutter either, but you know how people say that sometimes things happen in slow motion? Like when a car crashes or when you drop a kitchen knife toward your foot?

"Well, I'm sure time actually did slow down for me at that moment. One second I was driving along at a pace, and everything was a blur. There was rain and wind and car lights and people and traffic and leaves blowing across the road, and the next second, like something from *The Matrix*, the rain stopped, and the mist in the car cleared from the window. And there in the rain standing just beside the entrance to an empty bus shelter was what could only be described as a vision. She was there again! It was the girl in the red cloak. The girl who, for some yet undisclosed reason, stood away from everyone else outside of the bus shelter instead of taking its protection from the rain.

"She would stand alone in the same spot every day in the same inadequate coat regardless of the weather. She would hide her face with her hood even in the summer. She would stand and look straight out across the road at what only she could see. The girl with the thousand-yard stare!

"Before I had time to think, I had stopped the car, leaned across to the passenger door handle, and shoved open the door. And then she was in, and we were moving again. What the hell had I just done?

"No one has ever accused me of being an impulsive person. I put safety first every time and the words 'no thanks, I will just have the omelette' might as well be tattooed on my forehead. So did I know she had missed the last bus to college that day? Or did I feel impulsive because of the news I had just been given? Did I feel sorry for her because of the weather? Or did I see her and think of my daughter, Emma?

"Who knows why I stopped the car? I had never picked up a hitchhiker in my life, and she wasn't even hitchhiking. In my mind, people who pick up hitchhikers fall into two categories, neither of which I fit into at all. The first category is for people who were 'young once' and hitched lifts with strangers, see no danger in it, and feel they have to 'pay it back.' Those people don't see how weird they look to every normal person. They have an obligation to the hitchhiking community.

"I strongly suspect that there is an actual community, by the way. Probably based somewhere in Texas or Holland. I think they have regular meetings to discuss the best method of thumbing. They probably argue with those who bring the entire community into disrepute by shouting at the cars that fail to pick them up, therefore giving the next 'thumber' a lower chance of success. The second category is for paedos. No, but seriously, it's just a bit weird and creepy and *so* not me.

"Even if you know the person, you should make an excuse to avoid picking him or her up. Use a hand gesture as if to say, 'I am turning off at the next junction. I am not going your way—sorry.' Put the sun visor down and pretend to be squinting. Sunglasses are perfect, as you can pretend you didn't see the hitchhiker.

"Whatever it takes, don't stop. If you do, you will be looked upon as a paedo or a weirdo and everyone coming the other way will see you and say so. There are the hiders to watch out for too—don't forget them.

"The hitcher who the other hitchers think is the best at it will stand with his thumb raised up straight. When a car stops, out jump all of his mates. Then there's the repeat effect. Do you know, Peter, about the repeat effect? You pick up the hitcher, and then he's there the next day and the next day. He lives at the end of your road, he works near your work, he doesn't have a car, and you do. You know what I mean?

"So you pick him up on day one, and then how the hell do you drive past him on day two? And he's there on the way home, and now you're in a car share for the rest of your working life. And every single day he is beside you, you become more and more angry. After all, you have bills and rent to pay, and you bought a car and pay for the fuel, the insurance, and the maintenance, and he lives with his mum and has no bills. And you're his free ride. He's got more disposable income than you do now, and he's down at the pub every night getting off with girls that should be with you, and he's laughing at you.

"I know someone who that happened to. He actually pretended he had sold his car. He cycled to work for three months until he was sure that the parasite had a new host and that the graft had taken. No! Don't do it. Never. Ever!

"'This is all new,' I thought. I had not only picked up my first ever hitchhiker, but I had also picked up a woman! Shit! I had often seen her out of the corner of my eye and had wondered what she was looking at. In reality, I knew she probably wasn't looking at anything and was instead transfixed—lost in something—and that made her much more intriguing.

"Now this is going to sound a bit creepy, but I had imagined picking her up before. I had wondered what it would be like to be that person—that person who picks up hitchhikers. I had wondered what it would be like to have her sitting next to me. I had wondered what it would be like to be a very happily married man sitting next to a mysterious young girl. What would I say to her?

"I had wondered what would happen if I inadvertently touched her coat as I changed gears. I would apologize, and it would not have been on purpose you understand, but would she think I was trying it on? Would the car share become a regular thing? With the repeat effect and all. And what would people who saw us say? What would I say to my wife?

"I knew it would be innocent. I do know myself well enough to know I would never do anything like that. I wouldn't even think about it, but what would I say to my wife? And would she believe me when I said it was completely innocent? And it would be, by the way, but would it look innocent? Would it be nice to have company on my tedious commute each weekday? Or would it become awkward, and would I soon regret having started something I wasn't able to stop?

"Would we become friends and see each other at the farmers' market on Sunday and say hi? Would my friends wait until she had gone and then grab my arm and say, in a you-jammy-bastard way, 'How the hell do you know her?' Would I then smile and say, 'She's just a friend'? And would they reply, 'You old sly dog, you'? And I would just leave them thinking that I was an old sly dog even though I wasn't?

"As you can guess, I had thought about it a lot, and I had thought that I would never, ever actually stop and offer her—or anyone else, for that matter—a lift. But I had allowed myself to imagine it, and even that scared me. Hell, I even worried people would find out I had imagined it.

"As it turned out, none of that was relevant on the first occasion, because although it did become a regular thing (and I will get to that), on that first rainy morning in March, I was in a complete daze. I was in more than a daze. I was in a dream state.

"I had been given the diagnosis I had suspected would come, and yet it had hit me like a bolt from the blue. I thought I would be ready for the news, but I went to bits. I drove, and I stopped, and I drove, and she must have gotten in, but it didn't register. I said nothing and neither did she, as far as I know. It took me forty-five minutes to get to work, and she must have gotten out, and I must have parked and gone to work. I must have gone home that day, but I don't recall anything.

"In fact, I don't recall anything that happened for a few days after that, except for the fact that every morning I drove, stopped, and drove again, and she was in my car!

"I already know what you're thinking. 'Slippery slope. Whoa there, cowboy. What are you getting yourself involved in?' But it wasn't like that.

"I was in a catatonic state, and she was just staring straight ahead. That's how it was every day for weeks. I am sure now that not one word was spoken. Not ever. Not 'hello' or 'good-bye.' It seems strange now, but it felt normal to both of us at the time. It was comfortable, I think. It was not uncomfortable—I can say that.

"And neither of us had ever said a word. I shit you not. Not ever. We never had the radio on either because it was broken. And it was OK like that. I mean, it was OK for both of us. I personally don't recall thinking about the silence at all. It just was like that. Neither of us had anything to say. And that went on for months.

"I recall now that it was a very wet spring and that the rain would bounce off of the road and off of the cars in front us day after day. That made it hard to see. I was constantly wiping the inside of the front window, fiddling with the settings, adjusting my seat, trying to get the radio to work, and trying to see where I was going.

"It's only now that I recall that she kept her hood up the entire time. Come to think of it, she never so much as shifted in her seat. She never turned her head or wiped her nose or fiddled with her hair. She never took her eyes off of the horizon or so much as un-crossed her arms the entire time.

"Then before I knew what happened, it was nearly summer, we were stopped at a traffic light and people were in shorts and skirts. It was warm, and she still had her hood up, and people were crossing the street in front of us. And she said, 'Look at that asshole!'"

CHAPTER 6

BUMMER

———

J AMES HAD ONLY JUST BEGUN his fantastic story and
I was already feeling like it would be time to head
back to New York too soon. Day three in rainy old
England was much like the others had been. I got up
late with a hangover and staggered down to a breakfast of ham, eggs, toast, and tea—it was just like when
I was a teenager.

Mum was waiting for me and pretending she
hadn't been waiting as if it was normal for me to get
up at eleven every day. I guess she wanted to make it
like the old times, and Dad didn't complain too much
about my drinking and late nights at the pub for fear
of Mum kicking him under the table. After breakfast,
I walked the dog, and then Dad pried into my life with
questions about my job which were met with more
kicks under the metaphoric table from Mum. One
morning I remarked about how pleasant it was to walk
the dog with a hangover, and Dad said that Benjie

didn't drink. His attempted humor was met with an inevitable glare from Mum.

Later, I went back to sleep for an hour before dinner, then finally I got away and raced to the pub—only to find that James was not there. The pub was busy. In fact, there were few empty chairs, but there were two barstools in our usual spot with coats over them. As I approached the bar and began to order a beer, a friendly voice came from behind the toilet door. It said, "I'll get that," and to my relief it was James. He was there after all, and the two barstools with coats on them were ours.

We sat, and James inquired about my family, which was a nice gesture. I told him about Mum and Dad and about how I had just called my wife, who had told me off for going to the pub three nights in a row. Sandi and the girls didn't come for Christmas that year, I don't recall why, but some years they just didn't. School performances or the flu? Something like that. A few years ago it was just me and the girls because Sandi was in Florida for what felt like the entire month of December. She was covering the story about that serial killer who targeted old black female schoolteachers. He was eventually caught when his own mum found a severed hand in his bedside drawer.

So James and I had a few beers, and we chatted about life and love and stuff like that. And then just as

I was going to have to inquire about the girl he picked up, I didn't have to.

"As you can well imagine," James began. "After months of silence, her sudden outburst took me by surprise, to say the least. I mean, not a word for months, and then, 'Look at that asshole!' We sat there in my old Jag for a few seconds before what she had said registered, and then we both just burst out laughing. The ice was well and truly broken.

"I thought I would take a chance and see if I could drum up a conversation while I had her in a good mood and before the laughter abated.

"'My name is James Forester,' I said. 'Jim or James is fine with me.'"

"'Connie Blake,' she said, 'Well, Constancia really, but Connie for short.' That was the first time I noticed her faint accent. So I asked her where she was from, and she began to cry! Perhaps saying her original name triggered her off, but I think I have seen it before—it has probably happened to me before. Sometimes laughter slides so easily into tears.

"I don't know how or why it happened, but it didn't seem that unusual. Although it was a bit awkward, I left it alone, and then we continued in silence for a few more minutes.

"When she regained composure, I tried a completely different approach.

"'I have cancer,' I said, just like that. But no reply came back. Not a word.

"'Did you hear what I said?' I asked. But she was gone again. She had drifted off into a world of her own without a second's notice. Eventually, she wiped away the tears but said nothing. You see, she has this amazing 'thousand-yard' stare. It's like something out of a Hitchcock movie. She just can't see or hear or function when she slides away. She is gone, and although I haven't tried physically shaking her, I doubt it would bring her back.

"Eventually, she returned with a big sudden shiver, and I said, 'Connie, that's a nice name.' I tried not to make her cry again because we were nearing the university.

"As far as I remember, we didn't say anything on the way home until we neared her stop. Then she said, 'Cancer. How bad?'

"And I said, 'Not good.'

"And she said, 'Bummer!'

"And we both laughed, only that time it was my laughter that turned into tears, but I think she was getting out of the car by then, thank God."

"It was probably the first time I had ever said the word 'cancer' out loud. I had talked around and about it with Laura, of course, but Jake, who was about twenty-four at the time, still lived with us, what with the price of property 'round here and the easy life he gets from his mum. So it was always in hushed tones, and although Jake knew about it, I had never actually used the word—you know, the big *C*—Cancer in front of him. We all want to shelter people we love from our worst moments, don't we? I knew Jake was old enough to understand, of course, but I still thought of him as my baby boy, and his mother still treated him like that. As for Laura, I didn't know how she was coping. I didn't know how I was coping. I just tried not to talk about it, and she tried to go along with that."

"We bottle stuff up in my house, Peter, and then blurt it out across the safety of the dinner table—like the time a few months after Connie and I started to chat, Jake was out, Laura was eating while reading a magazine at the same time and I told her Connie said I should talk to her about the cancer. To which Laura obviously replied 'Who the hell is Connie?' I said something like, 'You know, the girl I told you about,' but we both knew I hadn't told her about Connie. I hadn't mentioned her once—not ever.

Laura said that she had actually seen me driving past her one day with Connie in the car but that she had been too embarrassed to say anything. She was with a girlfriend at the time and she thought for sure her friend had seen us as well, and also a few days after that Jake told his mum that some friends at work had seen us and said that I was a sly old fox or something and he nearly got in a fight about it for God's sake!"

"Laura wasn't mad with me, Peter, her tone was more disappointed. She looked at me and said something like, 'Do you know what? If Connie said I should talk more, perhaps this was as good a time as any!'

"So I just said, 'I have cancer.' And Laura said 'I know!'

"We both just stood in the kitchen looking down awhile. And then I noticed that she was crying and I wasn't, and so I held her ever so gently as if she might break. And she cried, and I held her and said everything would be OK. But as usual, she could tell I was lying."

"We went to the oncologist again a few weeks later. They all talk about you as if you are not in the room. As if it's inevitable that you will go along their path. He highlighted things on charts and talked about lymph glands and blood count and probabilities and what he was going to do next. But all of that time I was thinking to myself, 'This is me he is talking about. This is my life and my decision.'

"I knew what it meant to do nothing and to have no treatment, but I thought that at least I would have some quality of life during what little time I had left. How naive I was—how selfish I was. How wrong I was! So I drove to work and back as usual, but as I said, I was in a dream world for the first few months.

"Connie and I had been driving one particular morning for about thirty minutes, and neither of us had said a word. She had something on her mind that she was wrestling with. It was different from when she would just drift away into her own world. She wanted to say something, and I desperately wanted her to spit it out. I watched her for what seemed like an eternity, willing her to say it, but we arrived too soon at the university gates as we inevitably did each day.

CHAPTER 7

BREAKDOWN

———

James. Summer 2004.

"About five months after I first gave Connie a lift, things began to change. We were still doing our usual route to and from Oxford each weekday. We had completed little if any conversation, but we had grown fond of each other's company without really knowing anything about each other. In fact, 'fond' is probably too strong a word. 'Comfortable,' perhaps?

"Some people you are comfortable with, and some people you are not. It's immediate, and no one knows why. Like when you sit on an airplane and the chap gets on last and sits next to you, and sometimes, in fact almost always, you hate each other immediately. Nothing is ever said, and you have no idea why you hate each other. You just sit there for hours trying to share an armrest without resulting to actual violence. But very occasionally, it's almost the same in that nothing is said out loud, but there is no hatred at all. Sometimes you even think that the armrest sharer is quite a nice guy, although you don't say it. Well, it must have been like that. We got along without communication. I knew she was called Connie Blake and that she used to live quite near to me on the opposite side of the river.

"She of course knew my name and where I worked, roughly where I lived, and I am sure at times I rambled on about Laura and Jake. I talked a bit about my cancer and about the visits to the hospital without elaborating too much. She did not reply. She had 'gone into her shell' again, but I got the impression that she was sort of listening, maybe with a bit of sympathy. She had at least removed the hood from her head, and I could see her amazing jet-black hair. For the first time, I could see her face, and so could passersby. She was stunning in a way that was ridiculous.

"The fact that I was driving her to university boosted my ego in a proud-dad type of way. I doubt anyone on the street ever looked at me—they only saw Connie, and that was fine too, I guess. Weeks before when my wife had asked about Connie, I had said that she was strange, damaged, withdrawn, and almost sinister. I had said lots of things that were unfounded.

"When I was prompted by Laura, I said I had no idea if she was pretty or not, because in truth, I hadn't really looked at her. I wasn't deliberately trying to say that she was ugly or weird, but I am sure I gave that impression to Laura because from then on she would refer to her as my 'goth' friend or that 'emo' girl.

"I mentioned once that Connie had a big thumb ring which looked like a black skull on her left hand, and from then on, Laura would say 'How's lord of the rings?'

"I left it like that on purpose after I knew the truth because I didn't have the guts to tell Laura I was driving a goddess every day. And so for all of that time, I guess I did nothing to change Laura's mental picture of Connie.

"You can imagine my shock then when one Friday morning I broke down. Not only did I break down, but Connie also had an exam that morning, and I didn't have breakdown assistance. Laura was on her way into town to meet her mum, Penny, to do whatever it is women do.

"Laura answered her mobile after two attempts, and she was right there. I told her on the phone that I had broken down, but by then she could see. She had hung up and was pulling in behind me.

"Laura got out of her car and was standing at the back of mine with me and she said something like, 'Are you OK, James? What's wrong with the car? I've got to go, baby. I'm meeting my mum. It's her birthday, remember?'

"But every time she said a sentence, she tailed off at the end as if she was completely taken aback by something. And each time her words petered out, I glanced sideways to see what she was distracted by. And then I knew what it was! Connie had emerged from the passenger seat.

"Like only people with her presence can, she turned to look our way in what seemed to be slow motion. She turned just as the sun came out and as the wind tossed her hair. The wind actually tossed her long black perfectly curled hair. I promise you I thought I could hear the song 'Dream Weaver' by Gary Wright!

"I would not have been surprised if white doves had flown up from behind her or if she had somehow set off a huge fireworks display. And Laura thought the exact same thing. I could tell she did by the way she froze and by the way her jaw dropped slowly.

"That was the first time I truly knew how stunning Connie was, and trust me, so did Laura. The wind actually tossed her hair, and I thought Laura was going to pass out. As marriage-defining awkward silences go, I've had worse. No, I haven't. It was a big one, to say the least. Connie, as usual, was not going to say anything. I think she had only gotten out of the car to go catch the bus, seeing as she had the exam and all.

"But Laura just stood there openmouthed for ages until I finally said, 'Laura, Laura!' I thought I was going to have to click my fingers in front of her face. 'This is Connie. Connie, this is Laura,' I said. Still nothing.

"Eventually, and I can't remember what she actually said, Laura spoke. And the whole time she was looking back and forth from Connie to me. She said stuff like, 'It's so nice to finally meet you,' and, 'You're not at all how James described you.' And then when she let go of Connie's hand, she just fixed on me and gave me the look. The 'you and I will have words later' look.

"I swiftly moved things along and tried to make it less awkward by talking about the car, but it was clear to both of them that I was rambling, as I know nothing about cars during the best of times. I remembered that Connie had the exam, Laura had to meet her mum, and I could stay and wait for the garage truck. And like that, Connie was in Laura's car, and they were gone. I will never forget the look on Laura's face as she pulled away. She looked right at me, and I could tell she wanted to shake her head even though she didn't do it.

"I waited for the tow truck to come, and I waited a long time. Then the phone rang, and it was Laura. She started to say, 'What the fu—,' but she had only gotten to the *f* when the tow truck driver said, 'Hey, mister,' for the third time. So I just said, 'I'll call you back,' and hung up. Saved by the bell! But it only delayed the inevitable, which I was sort of ready for, really. I mean, Laura had known there was nothing going on, I am sure she knows me well enough by now, but if she ever had any doubts, they were gone once she took one look at Connie. It was thankfully clear for all to see that we were more like father and daughter than anything else and again I was grateful for that. My life was complicated enough now without any funny business thank you very much. I did still enjoy the looks people gave me though.

"Once I got a chance I called Laura straight back, and she was angry about my hanging up on her, but after I explained about the hovering and prodding truck driver, she moved on to the elephant in the room. To my relief, I could hear that she had a smile on her face. Boy, was it a relief. I wasn't ready for a fight over nothing, and I had nothing of any consequence to explain.

"Laura said, 'So how's lord of the rings, then?' We both laughed. 'I'll see you later,' she said, and with a chuckle, she hung up."

———

"Some time later when I was having a round of chemotherapy, Laura stood in as Connie's chauffeur for the week. I told Connie what was happening and asked her if she was going to be OK with Laura driving her each day instead of me. She really never said yes or no. For whatever reason, I said that Laura goes that way each day anyway, but Connie probably knew that wasn't true. As she hadn't actually agreed to the temporary change in drivers, I was glad to hear that she got in the car with Laura each day. I thought Laura would have to do most of the talking, so I gave her some strict dos and don'ts. I looked forward to hearing the inevitably one-sided conversations each evening.

"Laura was hooked immediately and would wait in the car to deliver Connie home again each evening.

"One night, Laura said, 'She told me she is originally from Portugal and that she plans to go back there one day.' Laura said it as if they had been chitchatting.

"'Bloody hell, that's more than she has told me in months,' I replied, my pride dented. 'I thought I was getting somewhere with her,' I said, but Laura just shrugged as if to say that you've either got it or you don't.

———

"So once I was back at the wheel and armed with the new knowledge of Connie's conversational skills, I wanted to ask her a question or two of my own.

"'If you go back to visit Portugal, what will you do first?' I asked. I of course thought she would say something like she wanted to go to the beach or to the village she was born in or to visit distant relations. So I was knocked off my feet when she quickly replied.

"'I want to know why my mother and father sold me to be a slave! When I was a little girl, I was sold to a bad man, who then sold me to another. And when I was old enough, I was sold to the worst man. A man who had sex with children and who took money from other men to have sex with children. In this country. In your country.'

"I could hear that her Portuguese accent was even stronger than I had imagined it was going to be. I could hear, too, that those words had never been spoken before. Her face never turned to look at me, and her voice was not filled with anger or bitterness but with disgust and revolution. I tried to ask her something, but what can you say to that? And so I said nothing. Then I was the one with the thousand-yard stare. I was the one completely lost for meaningful words. I was the one drifting off to view unimaginable horrors. I was the one with tears in my eyes.

"All that time, I had been filled to the brim with self-pity. I had wasted all of those weeks saying nothing and thinking of myself—thinking of my lot and of my hand in the cruel game of life. Then all I could do was blow air out of my nose and shake my head. Perspective or what?"

CHAPTER 8

SANDI

———

IT WAS MY LAST NIGHT in England, and I was keen to get back home to New York. My boss had been on the phone to me about a crazy Japanese client of mine who had shot his wife on Christmas day. So I clearly had stuff to get back to and it goes without saying that I was missing Sandi and my two girls so much. Not seeing them at Christmas time was really too much, and I was sure this would be the last time I would do this trip alone.

Still I was here and I had better make the best of it, so as I had done for the last three nights, I rushed off to the pub after dinner to hopefully get the final installment from my newfound friend. Only James wasn't there, and he never showed up. I asked the bar staff if James had been in, but he hadn't. I knew it was futile to ask where he lived because we barely knew each other and I was never going to march around the guy's house and demand to know what had happened in the end.

So that was that. I sat in the pub at my usual stool and resented anyone who sat on the one to my right. I stayed there all night, but all I got for my trouble was yet another hangover.

So the next morning once my good-byes were done, I headed off to Heathrow in the back of the taxi. Then it was me in a world of my own. The rain lashed against the car and the wind blew leaves across the road. I sat leaning against the side window in a trance. I was much the same all the way home. I don't recall the airline food or the woman who sat next to me for eight hours, but I do recall staring out of the window an awful lot.

Sandi met me at JFK, and I was much the same during the car ride to the apartment. In fact, I was much the same for some while until my work allowed me the time to truly do the story justice. I began to tell it with all of the details I could remember to Sandi, who, as you can imagine, was keen to know what had affected me so badly. She was in from the get-go, as we say out here, and she pressed me each evening for more. I began to remember small snippets I had forgotten about and details I had missed. And of course, she set about researching the players in my Shakespearean story.

Sandi used her skills as a journalist and her connections to help me investigate James and his incredible story. You see, although I was convinced he had told me the truth, it was so "out there" that Sandi took some persuading. At first, Sandi thought it was probably complete fiction. But once she had trawled the Internet and phoned the university pretending to be interested in enrollment, she knew that at least he was a real person with a wife, a son, a job, and a story, and she knew that the girl existed. So with our investigations and what James had told me, we began to piece together a pretty good picture of them all.

James Thomas Forester was just nineteen years old when he first met Laura. She was a tall, skinny, shy eighteen-year-old beauty from distant Italian lineage. Her grandparents had moved to England just before the First World War. James told me once that he knew the exact date when he first set eyes on Laura—2 September 1971. He mainly remembered it because they met at Laura's eighteenth birthday party, which was held at a posh hotel on the banks of the River Thames. That sounds more romantic than it actually was on account of the fact that Laura was the guest of honor and James was the drummer in the house band. Still, their eyes did meet across a crowded dance floor, and the attraction was mutual, instant, and binding.

He was classically British: rugged but not charming, and handsome but not pretty. He was the leader of his pack, but he was polite and soft-spoken. He was well bred but not squeaky clean. She was dark, sexy, and striking—a smoky Mediterranean type. She was imposing but shy and demure. You know how those poor supermodels never get asked out? Everyone expects them to either already be with Brad Pitt or to say no to an invite because they are leagues above everyone else. Therefore, they never get hit on. Well, Laura was like one of those girls for sure. Thankfully, James was just about in her league—or, because he was the drummer in the band and had had a couple of beers, he thought he was at the time. By all accounts, they were an item immediately.

Unbeknownst to them, they lived just streets apart. Laura still lived at home with her mum and dad, Penny and Alfie Moretti, in a small smart house just off the park. James was by then in his first year at university and had his own place in town. She thought he was handsome and intellectual, and he certainly was a bright spark in class. Economics, he would one day tell her, is like accounting with the ability to monetize. She never really understood what he meant and assumed he had gotten the catchphrase from a Charlie Sheen film or something.

It is certainly true that he did monetize his knowledge of economics by investing in start-up companies (one of which paid off) while still having a critically acclaimed career as an Oxford professor. OK, we did discover that his father's money gave him a head start, but his brain played a big role in the process. They were married in Saint Mary's Church in Henley-on-Thames on 1 August 1975.

Henley-on-Thames is a small town not far from Oxford. It's the place where the university crew team has its training headquarters. That very rowing club-house, "Leander," was the illustrious venue for the happy couple's wedding reception thanks to an influential uncle who gladly stepped up. A very posh event indeed, both Laura and James must have been delighted that they didn't have to pay for it. They went off on a honeymoon in Cornwall for a few days and then settled down in the spare room of Laura's parents' house in Oxford.

Although we tried to find some points of interest in the next few years of James's and Laura's life, Sandi and I failed. I'm not saying they disappeared, but they lived life under the radar. He ended his studies, received a job offer at the same university, and moved almost seamlessly into his career before eventually becoming a professor of economics.

Laura continued her only job after graduation at Brightwaters Estate Agents until the week before the twins were born. They saved and bought their first house not far away from everything and everyone and had a simple life. There were no flashy cars or scandalous affairs; they led a simple, ordinary life that some would call mundane.

So we wrongly decided that their lives had gone smoothly and turned our attention to the girl. That was a much more difficult investigation because she was an immigrant and an orphan. Once we found out her full name from her school records, we were able to trace her past to greater depths than we had first thought was possible. When James met her, she was going by the name of Connie Blake. "Blake" was her adopted parents' last name, but her full name was—or at least would have been if she had stayed in Portugal— Constancia Maria Costa-Santos de Alameda. The Portuguese get such long names because they take names from both parents and, at times, from their grandparents.

So we knew that she was originally from Portugal and that her mother was from a small village near Estoril, a hand-to-mouth community of poor fishermen. The sort of place where dirt roads still exist to this day and a place where small boats sit in sunscorched bays. It is not a typical tourist destination— it's not on the popular coast, but it's also not deserted or completely forgotten.

We never traced her father—he wasn't listed on any paperwork we could find, and by all accounts, he remains completely unknown. Sadly, when Connie was just a baby, her mother dispatched her to live with an elderly uncle in Lisbon until she was five. We couldn't discover her mother's reason for doing so.

Then, again for unknown reasons, she was dispatched to live in England with another ill-equipped friend or relative. Finally, she was officially adopted by a middle-aged childless couple named Alan and Hillary Blake.

Connie was a very bright girl even at a young age. The Blakes were high achievers. Both had illustrious careers in the city in public offices. Connie excelled at school and was to study physics at Oxford and, I am sure, to go on to great things. However, in school, she was withdrawn, which was probably attributed to the language barrier and to her adoption.

Mr. and Mrs. Blake were a quiet couple from a small village near Reading. They did very well for themselves and retired early to their huge dream house in the best part of well-to-do Marlow. It was a magnificent private estate on the banks of the river, and it was complete with a boathouse and a croquet lawn.

For whatever reason, they were not able to have children of their own. Perhaps they waited until after their careers and it was too late? Regardless, they were soon blessed with the daughter they had always dreamed of—Constancia. "Connie," as they immediately called her, was then just ten years old. By all accounts, they were strict parents, and in a short time they managed to turn her into a reclusive and withdrawn teenager. She was gifted and bright but not equipped for the outside world.

In time, we had done all that we could do. We had learned all we could about the story and the people—or so we thought—and it was time to leave it alone. We resigned ourselves to the fact that we would never know what had become of Connie, James, and Laura. We would never find out what had happened in the end—at least that's what we thought before Christmas came around again!

CHAPTER 9

EMMA.

———

"WHERE THE HELL WERE YOU last year?" I said as I slapped his back and he spilled his drink.

"Hello, Peter. Look what the cat dragged in!" James tried to say while wiping beer from his face. He acted as if he hadn't been expecting me, although I think he probably had been.

"Never mind that," I said. "Where were you on that Thursday evening? I sat on this very barstool all night, and you stood me up."

"Sorry, mate," James said as he rose to greet me. No explanation was demanded or given, so we just laughed, shook hands, and clinked glasses for the next hour or so.

It was ten o'clock on my first night back in the United Kingdom, and it was Christmas Eve, so we had a couple of beers. And then we shared a very big hug before leaving the warmth of the pub fire and heading out through the unstoppable rain and wind to our families. I purposely didn't ask too many questions about Connie or Laura or his health. I didn't want him to know that I had come all that way a year later to do exactly that. I kept stopping myself from inquiring and instead made him promise to meet me on the barstools each night of the week as he had done the last year. Much to my relief, he agreed warmly, and we parted with yet another handshake that turned into a hug.

So off we both went to have Christmas with our families. I, of course, couldn't wait to get to the pub each night after Boxing Day. It went as I had planned it: Sandi stayed at my mum's with Dad and the kids because someone had to while I made my usual excuses. I had the added bonus of my wife's blessing, and so I went to the pub around eight thirty each night until we returned to New York on January second. New Year's Eve was the only exception, but I will get to that later. I had four nights to catch up with James and, of course, to have a few beers.

I asked him how he was doing, and he assumed that I was asking how the cancer was doing. He said it was a long story and that it had been a hell of a year. James looked better than he had when I had last seen him. He was physically thinner and he had shorter hair, but overall he looked much healthier.

"As always, Laura was right about the advances in research and treatment." James began. "Things have moved forward even in the past year. I gladly accepted the invitation to go on one of those drugs trials— or maybe I was on the placebo? Anyway, it worked, I think. I feel OK, to be honest. Still got cancer of course, although they tell me I am in remission and I feel OK. It turns out it's the best place to get it if you have to get it. In the nuts, I mean. It turns out it's one of the easiest to treat or has a very high survival rate at least. I could have done with believing that at the start, but when you hear the *C* word…well, you know?

"Anyway, I am so glad you are back, Peter. So much has happened since we last met and I truly enjoy confiding in you. It's so much easier than with family. I hope you don't mind. I know I left you with some parts of a story last year—perhaps I did that on purpose so you would come back. Anyway, I'm glad that you're here. It's nice to see you.

"It wasn't all smooth sailing, but I think we are through the worst. For sure, we have put some stuff to bed. I never told you the truth, Peter. The real reason I was here every night last year? I was here because you were here!

"On that first night, I had had a tiff with Laura, and she had gone home after dinner, so I stayed in the pub. You walked up next to me and we got on and chatted, and I said some stuff I hadn't ever said out loud before. You remember the first night? I listened to you make a twat of yourself to the bar staff. And I listened to every word. You told the girl behind the bar that you were a hotshot lawyer."

"Attorney, I said!"

"Whatever," James said. "And you said that your wife was a journalist for a fancy-pants newspaper."

"I didn't say fancy pants."

"I know. I'm pulling your leg. But I was listening and thinking, and I decided it was time. Time I told someone—someone who might be able to help or at least understand, someone other than Laura—about my cancer and how I felt and about Connie and most of all about my beautiful daughter Emma who was taken from us years ago. So you see, in a way I chose you. And now you are involved."

"Involved in what?" I asked, hoping I was involved in something.

I reminded myself that I was an attorney and that Sandi was a journalist. Maybe he saw some way my knowledge of the law could help him or that we could get some publicity if something went wrong—anyway, it was all very intriguing. So as usual, I shut up and let James do all of the talking.

"During the days after Connie first told me about her abuse, I was naturally stunned, but for once, I was not stunned into silence. I had immense anger. I had good reasons to be angry, and I had bottled up my anger for too long. Do you know what was on my mind when I was late for work that day—the day I got the bad news and picked Connie up? Do you know what was on my mind, Peter? Do you know why I picked her up? It was because of Emma. Do you remember what I said to you? I said, 'It was the second time in my life that I had been late for work, the first being when Laura gave birth to the twins twenty-five years ago.'

"You never asked me about my kids, and I thank you for that. I think I told you that Jake is doing great, but I didn't tell you about my poor Emma."

James broke down, and I didn't know what to do. I sort of hugged him in a manly way and looked around. He shook it off quickly, thank God, and was determined to continue.

"It was Sunday, June twenty-eighth, 1987. Emma and Jake's tenth birthday party. The house was full of kids in party hats and cake and music. It was warm out, and my two had gotten a trampoline for their birthday. It was their favorite thing. They were on it with their friends all afternoon.

"Did you know, Peter"—James said, changing the subject to see if I was still listening—"June twenty-eighth was the day the First World War started? Well, it was the day when that chap got assassinated, which lead to the First World War. I don't know why I know that."

"Archduke Franz Ferdinand," I said.

"That's right," James said.

"I know! Now stop stalling."

"OK, OK. Well, anyway, here goes.

"Emma was in the back garden. Everyone else had gone home or was in the house, and we were washing dishes and the television was on loud, and people were saying good-bye. And then, just like that, Emma was gone. At first, we thought she had fallen off the trampoline, which horrified us. We quickly rushed into the garden. But she wasn't there.

"She wasn't anywhere. I can't describe the sheer panic. It rises. You can't stop it. It rises and rises. First, we phoned everyone who was at the party and asked if she had gone home with them for some reason. We thought maybe she was playing hide-and-seek. It rises and rises, and you collapse.

"But Jake was there, and some of the other kids and their parents were still there, so I tried to hold it together. But people were running 'round and shouting her name. Then our neighbors were out, and it was getting dark, and people were calling her name. Before long, the police were there, and Laura was with me, and Jake was with neighbors in the kitchen. I could hear him screaming for his sister. I could hear him over Laura, who was out of control with despair. I can still hear him now.

"No one slept—not for weeks—and in the end our doctors put us on stuff we were unable to fight. We searched everywhere for days. It was on the news every minute. We did a press conference and pleaded for her safe return. We were all together in the kitchen when she was taken. Otherwise, I'm sure they would have interviewed the next-door neighbors and me. Everyone else was under suspicion.

"The entire village was out with dogs and sticks and torches. It went on for months, but my Emma, my beautiful perfect little thing, was never seen again.

"The loss is unimaginable. Indescribable. The heart won't mend, and I didn't want it to for fear I would forget about her in a way.

"I was trapped, and I couldn't move on until she came back. I couldn't think of what she was going through for fear that I would just die. I hoped that she was dead rather than being held by a monster, but I couldn't even say that to myself for fear that it would come true. I wanted her back, or at least I wanted to know where she was or whether she was alive or dead. If it turned out she was dead, I wanted her body back.

"I didn't think of the person who took her until much later on. I tried not to give him the satisfaction of knowing that I was thinking about him at all. I even suppressed thoughts of what I would have done to him in case he did find out and did something to Emma in retaliation. It just went on and on.

"About a mile from the back of our house, there is a main road, and from that road a track runs behind my house and down to the river. A few people walk their dogs there, and it comes within three feet of our back garden. The trampoline was quite close to the hedge, but it was only fifty feet or so from the kitchen window. How had it happened?

"I tried to understand the mind of the man who took my daughter so I could find her, and the police had specialist profilers doing the same. They think she was tempted by a man—probably a man with a dog. She walked toward the hedge, and then bang! He struck. It probably took as long as it takes to say it.

"One second she was on the trampoline having the best birthday ever, and the next second she saw a cute fluffy dog, and the man saw my beautiful girl in full flight—full of joy and life at the top of each bounce. And he couldn't stop himself.

"Maybe he had gone for a walk in the lane in the hopes of seeing a child on his or her own, and then the opportunity was there, and his hand reached, and she was gone. The police dogs tracked Emma through a section of the hedge that had been trampled a little and down the lane toward the river which was to the east about four houses away. At that river bank the trail went cold. So police concluded that Emma was probably taken from there by boat. As it was near the regatta week there had been many boats about that fateful day and no one would have stood out from the crowd.

"The police asked up and down our street. They poked their noses in every houseboat, canal boat, and river barge. At that time of year, they were moored up along all the banks almost end to end in places. Naturally, they also spoke to the house owners whose gardens and boathouses were directly on the river's edge. That is where they found the boat some days later. And it had been 'borrowed' while the nice family who owned it had been away.

"It must have been getting dark by the time he got her to the river to a waiting boat. She must have been so scared. For the first few days at least, the police were fairly confident that she would soon be found, probably at a neighbor's or friend's house. But when that didn't pan out, they started to look properly.

"By then, she could have been anywhere in the country or even abroad. Emma was gone. It hit all of us hard. It hit Jake worst of all. His birthday came and went each year and only served as a reminder of what we had all lost. We couldn't move from that house because we didn't want her to come back through the hedge to find strangers living there. So we stayed and rebuilt our lives and the house. We changed the kitchen so it no longer looked out over the garden, and the trampoline was long gone. The garden was paved over so I didn't have to spend any time out there. Every time I went out near where the trampoline used to be, I thought I could smell men's aftershave. We didn't keep her bedroom as a shrine—well, we did for a few years, but one day Jake was just standing in there crying, and so enough was enough.

"I was in tears when I removed the pink Barbie pony wallpaper with loving care. The spare roll is still in the loft. Emma's room will always be her room, and we all refer to it as just that. But now it's a cozy den for film nights and quiet reading.

"I still go in there a lot when no one is home. I cry and hold her favorite teddy, and I just stand there looking out the window at the garden. I know it's not healthy. It serves no good at all. I know. I just can't stop myself. And I think Laura does the same when Jake and I are out. Even when we stopped searching we never stopped hoping.

"Time flies by so fast, and before we knew it, Jake had his twentieth birthday barbeque in the same garden. The sadness has to be buried deeper each year to help the others.

"Back in those days, forensic sciences were actually pretty advanced. I mean, eighty-seven is not sixty-seven, and the police painstakingly gathered DNA from the hedge through which bare arms had snatched Emma and from the boat where duct tape lay torn. There were no matches in any databases that existed at the time, and so the information was logged and stored, but the trail soon went cold. The investigators assigned to the case were superb people one and all. They never gave up. Occasionally a lead would come up but something promising never went anywhere.

"People were interviewed, of course, and sadly that list included friends, relatives, and neighbors. They all participated without complaint, and we never once suspected any of them.

"I was surprised to learn that my Emma was one of at least four girls of approximately the same age who were snatched away that year in the United Kingdom. That was slightly more than the previous year, but it was not an unusual total. There were also many more unexplained disappearances of girls of differing ages who might or might not have been runaways.

"The motive in every solved case was sexual, and in every conviction the child was dead and the perpetrator was white, male, and between twenty and forty-five years old. Most of the victims had known their attackers! We naturally feared the worst and tried to prepare for the worst, but if it never happened, what then? I mean, if we never found her or found out what had happened to her. What would we do then? We never gave up hope and thought about her every day. It was something we were going to have to live with for the rest of our lives. Time just passes you by somehow.

"Then a few years ago, I think it must have been spring of 2002 there was a knock at the door. For many years, whenever there was a knock at the door, we all stopped and looked at each other as if it would be the day Emma came home.

"The police had used an expert to do artist impressions of what she would look like as she got older, and I always had the latest one in my mind when I opened the door. It never was Emma at the door, though. That time, it was the other knock. The one we had dreaded for the first few years and then, sort of shamefully, had longed for. That time, it was the police.

"Three police officers, to be precise. One uniformed female officer, or WPC as they are affectionately referred to, one serving inspector, and the now-retired Mark Benson. Mark had been the original inspector in charge of the hunt for Emma and her abductor. He had become a family friend, and we have a lot to thank him for.

"'Hi, Mark,' I said, already shaking. 'Please come in, all of you. Please come in.'

"'James, how are you, mate? Nice to see you. This is WPC Wilkins and Inspector Isaac Ridatt. Isaac took over from me when I retired from the police force. Have you all met before?'

"'No, I don't think so,' Ridatt quickly said. 'Call me Zac—everyone does.'

"'Laura, Jake, I am so glad you are both here,' Mark said. 'We got the bastard.' Mark gestured to Inspector Ridatt.

"'Oh, yep. Sure,' Ridatt said. In a jolt, he reached into his shouldered bag.

"I knew what it was immediately, and I looked at Laura, who was stretching out her hand but was already falling apart at the seams. The bright, clean evidence bag was sealed tight and labeled 'Nineteen SF' in black marker. What was in it was as distinct as it was unforgettable.

"You see, the last pictures of Emma are all from her birthday party, of course. We have spent years clutching them and staring at them with love and despair. She loved that colorful new party dress. And we had it back. Finally, we had her back.

"'Where?' I asked as I looked back and forth between the three officers.

"'I can't tell you that yet, James. I apologize, but you must understand that there are procedures and safeguards,' Inspector Ridatt said in a kind but authoritative voice.

"'Where, Mark?' I tried again with more anger and hoped that Mark would answer instead of Inspector Ridatt.

"Ridatt started to say, 'We can't,' but Mark cut him off.

"'Liverpool.'

"'Inspector Benson!' Ridatt shouted even though he knew full well that Mark was no longer an inspector.

"'A terraced house. An ordinary terraced house on an ordinary street,' Mark said.

"'Mark, I must insist,' Ridatt said. But he knew he had no authority over Mark. Perhaps he shouldn't have been courteous enough to call Mark when the discovery had been made, but officers do that sort of thing, or at least they did back then. After all, it was a case that had consumed Mark's career, and he had not been retired from the force for long.

"Nowadays, I doubt they would take key evidence with them to the victim's parents' house, but I guess back then it was a courtesy and a simple way to confirm the identity of a victim.

"'A delivery driver about your age James. Under arrest, mate.' Mark said.

"'We've got him, sir, don't you worry,' Ridatt added as if he imagined that official police confirmation were required at this point.

"'What about Emma?' Laura asked.

"I hadn't thought to ask. I guess I already knew.

"'They have people taking the place apart now,' Mark said. 'This was in the wardrobe in the spare room along with many others like it,' he reluctantly said as he gestured toward the evidence bag. The bag was back in Ridatt's hands, much to his relief.

"'The guy has lived on his own in that house for years, and he has no kids. He just tried to take a little girl off the street in Glasgow in broad daylight. It's him all right. Don't you worry about that, Jim. We got the bastard for sure.'

"I think we all understood that it meant an awful lot to Mark to have that man locked up. It probably meant almost as much to him as it did to us. Mark had three young girls of his own, and he had inevitably taken our case to heart.

"'What about Emma? Is she there? Have you…,' Laura couldn't say the words, so she looked at me instead.

"'Have you found signs? Other than her dress, I mean. You know?' I asked.

"Mark looked down a bit and then explained that there was a hidden room where he had probably kept her but that she was no longer there.

"'There are no cellars or anything like that, but unfortunately it appears that the garden was regularly disturbed and that it's now been paved over. Neighbors have already confirmed that. As far as we know, he doesn't own or rent any other property. Inspector Ridatt interjected at this point to add that their initial look 'round the house and on the man's computer seemed to confirm all of their worst fears about what type of man he was and the things he was into.

"Laura finished by enquiring if the little girl from Glasgow was all right, which was so like Laura. Mark assured us that she was thankfully and with that the three of them left.

"They had a T.V. news helicopter over the bastards house the next day. God knows how these things leak out, but the twenty-four-hour news crews had more information about what was going on in Liverpool than we did. It didn't take long before white plastic tents obscured the view of the garden. We could see people in blue coveralls coming and going from the tents.

"On the day they dug up the garden, we began to get our hopes up. We thought it could be 'the day.' Inspector Ridatt invited us to Liverpool soon after the tents went up, but we declined. We just didn't feel up to it to start with. It took only thirty-six hours for the media to find us. They followed our every move. The police assigned an officer, a very pleasant young WPC, to stay with us all of the time. I couldn't have gone to work if I had wanted to. We were prisoners in our own home. Jake went to stay at a friend's house just a few doors down, and thankfully he was left alone.

"On the fourth day of the investigations at the Liverpool address, Inspector Ridatt was back at our house with a purpose.

"'We found a note,' he said. He did not give us time to prepare ourselves for what was about to come.

"They had found a scrap of a cardboard box that had been pushed through a gap in the wooden floorboards of the room they believed Emma was held in.

"As compassionately as possible, he held out a photocopy of what looked like a shred of a gray cardboard box. We immediately recognized the scribbled handwriting of our little girl. Laura just fell to her knees and screamed out. Her cry was like nothing I had ever heard before. It was a cry of pain which barely sounded human at all.

"Dear Mummy and Daddy, I miss you and want to come home. Can I come home soon? When you come to get me, can you bring horsey and blankey and Jake too? Please come soon. Emma. X O X O.

"Ridatt was bursting with something else, and he said, 'That's not all!'

"The cereal box that she had written the note on had a bar code on it as they all do, and it was on the other side of the note just visible on one edge. It was almost complete, and it was enough, at least, to determine the box's origins.

"'If Emma wrote this—' he began.

"'Of course she wrote this. It's her writing. I have some of her writing upstairs to compare the note to if you don't believe me. And she says 'Jake' and 'horsey' too.'

"Laura began to turn to retrieve Emma's schoolwork when Ridatt stopped her with another bombshell.

"'Mrs. Forester, we know Emma wrote this, but she wrote it three years after she disappeared.'"

CHAPTER 10

GONE SOUTH

―――

James. Christmas 2006.

"EMMA WAS TEN YEARS OLD when she was taken from us in the summer of 1987.

"She was snatched away by a twenty-nine-year-old single, white man. He was a man of whom astounded neighbors and relatives said 'wouldn't hurt a fly.' A man who was said to 'keep himself to himself.' A man with a face and now a name!

"After all of that time, we knew. We knew his face. His name, even his goddamned address! He looked like he could be the guy next door. A painter and decorator. He was somebody's son or brother. He was probably people's friend or teammate. This guy actually existed. He was no longer the nameless monster we had envisaged all these years. He was real. He lived and his name was Steve!

"I first saw his face in the paper a few days after he was charged. In fact, we didn't even know we had seen his face until it was all over the news at ten that night.

"I said to Laura, 'That's the bloke in the paper. I walked past the newsstand this morning and saw his face.' Now I almost felt cheated that I had seen him on the front cover of the newspaper but hadn't known who I was looking at. Laura had done something similar too. There he was, smiling at us from the ten o'clock news. The picture they used was like a still from an old holiday photo album. It must have been donated to the eager press by a friend or neighbor, no doubt. All of the other people in the photo were blacked out, of course. He had a bare chest and a beer in his hand. How dare he be a real person with friends, I thought. How dare he have a good time on a beach like a normal person.

"Then Laura was crying uncontrollably again. And then we were both crying and saying things like 'stop' and looking away. We must have thought of the same thing at the same time. When had that picture been taken? Had our little girl been locked in a dark cell somewhere while he was sunning himself? Had our precious, beautiful, scared baby girl been tied up somewhere cold and dark while Steve smiled into the lens?

"Then I thought about his chest hair and his tanned skin. Had that been pressed against my daughter's young body? Had his stubble and his disgusting mouth pressed against her lips? Had his hand, then tight 'round the beer glass, once been tight 'round her neck? It was all too much, and it never stopped. It still never stops. I see him every time I close my eyes. I see Emma locked in a room and him. And he is on her, and she is scared and crying out for me, and I can't reach her. Now that I have seen his picture, it is worse, not better. I see him in my mind, touching her and hurting her endlessly. His picture was on the news all of the time.

"Remember when I said I didn't dare think of harming him in case he found out, Peter? Well, now I can think of him, and I do. I think of him dead or dying in pain, and it's beautiful. It's therapeutic if not healthy I promise you. If I could, I would torture him. Like they do in the worst of the war movies. My wife goes to a therapist who says that those thoughts are negative and that it's damaging to hate him. She's a tree-hugging do-gooder called something like 'Miranda.' She fills Laura's head with all sorts of mumbo jumbo. I have to endure it each time Laura gets home. It may not help everyone to hate, but I like it. It suits me. I want to kill the bastard.

"I could do without his picture in my head all of the time, but the alternative is to stop thinking about it altogether. For me, that would be the same as no longer remembering Emma. I wouldn't ever want her to think I was going to let him get away with what he did to her. Well, I'm not. Not ever. Stupid bitch of a therapist—what does she know about hate, anyway? I know—more hate, which is unhelpful.

"But you have no idea what I would do to him if they let me. I have thoughts that are bad enough to get me arrested. I dream of burning his cock off and of slowly squeezing it in a vice. If they let me, I would gladly be the executioner, and I would mess it up on purpose to cause him as much suffering as possible. I know what people would say. It won't bring Emma back. Well, no shit. Trust me, I know that better than anyone. I would just enjoy torturing him until his eyes pop out of his skull. So there.

"They dug up the entire garden in Liverpool and found the body of a young girl. It was a cold dark Wednesday, and I was at work when Zac Ridatt came calling. I saw him through the window as he parked the car. I tried not to think. I tried to continue the lecture until the very moment he knocked on the door.

"Once we were in the privacy of my office, he said, 'It's not Emma.'

"'What?' I said.

"'It's not her, James. It's not. This poor little one was black. And young. Probably only about seven or eight, or so the forensic experts tell me.'

"'Yes!' I thought. Then I felt bad for the little black girl he had murdered and for her parents. But then I said 'yes' to myself again. Then I thought for a moment this meant that Emma might have still been alive. But I knew she really wasn't, and as soon as that, I was back to the feelings I had had for so long. I longed to know where she was. What had happened to her? Where had she been buried? And then I'd gone full circle in twenty seconds, and I wished that they had found Emma in the shallow grave under the patio in Liverpool. But it wasn't her.

"I went straight home to tell Laura. I watched as her face told the story of her emotions. I saw her go through the same twenty-second roller coaster of emotions I had gone through, and then we both slumped down on the sofa and held our heads in our hands, taking it all in. Digesting the possibility that Emma might have been alive. Knowing deep down she wasn't, but allowing ourselves the bliss of hope for a brief second before it was washed away once more.

"Our Emma was snatched away from us by Steven Andrew South of number five Chester Rise in Liverpool on the twenty-eighth of June nineteen eighty-seven. He was in our town that month painting a house not a mile away. The owners of the house had a thirty-foot riverboat. South used it without the owners' knowledge or consent while they were in Spain. The description of Steven South, which was given at interview to the police by the owners of the boat, turned out to be completely rubbish, but they

81

had only met South once when he visited the boat-house to quote for the work. South was long gone when they finally returned from their exotic holiday to find the painting work incomplete and their expensive boat well used.

"South was predominantly a freelance delivery driver, which meant that he had his own van. Businesses would call and give him stuff that needed to be delivered all around the United Kingdom. When work was hard to find, he turned his hand to painting and decorating. Later in life, he seemed to find an alternative Internet business that paid him very well. It paid well enough that he was able to travel extensively, but for some reason, he continued with his delivery van business when the occasion presented itself.

"By the time South was arrested, fifteen agonizing years had somehow gone by. We spent all those years waiting for news, but nothing other than Emma walking back in the front door or her body being discovered was going to put anything to rest. Even if she had been discovered, we wouldn't have had 'closure,' whatever that is. We would have had a trial to endure and a man to hate. A man to watch grow old in prison. A man still alive, locked away in a warm comfortable cell block while our daughter was dead. A man whose parole hearing we would have longed to go to—even if we had to wait for twenty years—so we could protest his release. A man who one day, God forbid, might have actually been released.

"Emma would have been about twenty-nine years old by now. It's hard to imagine her. I doubt we would recognize her. When will this ever end?

"It turns out the house in Liverpool gave up most of its secrets. The white-and-blue-suited good people of the forensic department did their jobs amazingly well, and we were constantly informed of the latest scientific finds, all of which would one day gang up on Steven South and his silence.

"Emma had been there all right. She had been there for at least three and a half years. Her hair, her nail clippings, and her chipped tooth were there. We even learned, believe it or not, the odd bit of information we could have done without. She became a woman while she was in that house. It was revealed to us delicately one day by a young female police officer that all the evidence suggested Emma was not permitted any sanitary products while at the Liverpool house. It is assumed probably because Steven South as a single man supposed to be living alone couldn't be seen to purchase that sort of thing without arising suspicion.

"It's so hard to ask the police questions without getting information you would rather not have. You want to know everything, as if that would help. As if that would fill in the gaps. We thought we would be closer to Emma if we knew more about her and about what she had gone through. But knowing more rarely did anything of the sort.

"In fact, it usually just added to the pain. The police tried to be tactful, but we asked the questions, and we had to expect the answers. Most the time, it was not pleasant."

CHAPTER 11

GLASGOW KISS

———

I AM SURE STEVEN SOUTH cares very little for the ter-
ror he causes. Imagine just how scared that little girl
must have been when he tried and almost succeeded in
snatching her from a Glasgow street. The papers soon
named her as Ellie McLeish. She was just twelve years
old and happily making her way home from school.

Put yourself in little Ellie's shoes for one moment
and imagine what it must have been like when Steven
South came to grab her away. Imagine you are her.
You're not exactly skipping, but you've had a great day.
Your friends at school voted you "star of the week,"
and your happiness shows in your walk. But then a
white van slows down next to you. The road is quiet.
No houses are nearby. Trees overhang this spot on
the sidewalk. You know not to talk to strangers, and
you're never getting in that van, no matter how many
sweets and puppies are in there.

But Steven South doesn't know that. Steven South is up to his old tricks again. Only this time, he is fat, old, slow, and reckless, and you're a junior judo champion and much bigger than you should be at your age. How could he know that, though? At the age of forty-four, he probably would have bet on himself against you any day. All he sees is a little girl in a primary school uniform alone on a quiet road. Skirts have gotten shorter and tighter since he started this sort of thing, and girls wear their socks pulled right up over their knees because of the cold. He's like a bee drawn to honey.

Then before he knows what has hit him, he is folded up on the ground and can't get up and can't move, and you have him in a choke hold and you are screaming out for help. A car comes toward you. You hope the car will see you on the ground by the van. You wonder how long you can hold on for.

He wants to get away—make no mistake about it. He's biting now. That just makes you angry. Choke him more. Scream more. There's more traffic now. You pray that someone will see you.

He is up. Your strength almost gone. He stands as if to run. He hesitates to turn to the van. You are under the van now. You are hiding and cowering. Instinctively, you grab at his leg as he tries to get in. He shakes and kicks, but you hold on for your life as the engine starts. The wheels are close, and your arm is sore. You pull, and you slide on the asphalt.

His right leg is still sticking out of the van. The hand brake is back on now. He is out again and dragging you from under the van. The side door slides open, and you are bundled in. He is panicking now. Almost raging out of control. Making mistakes. You kick at the perfect moment, and his nose explodes. He falls back. You are out and down the street running as fast as you can. You look back. A lorry appeared at just the right moment, in time to see you escape from the van, in time to act. Tires screech, the lorry swerves over to block it and the van is trapped. South runs, a child screams "rape," and all hell breaks loose. He knows this is it.

The lorry driver runs after him, and the passersby join in. South is surrounded now. The lynch mob shouts, screams, and swears. He lunges for freedom one last time, but it's over. It's all over for Steven South. Thanks to you.

———

The police arrived in minutes. At first, no one knew what had taken place. No one knew the magnitude of it all. They had no idea that they had a serial killer of children on their hands. If they had, I'm sure they would have held him tighter.

He might have even been the first person executed in public in two hundred years if the people of that part of Glasgow had known who they had had a hold of. But then the law showed up. There was a lot of shouting and screaming. There was a lot of testosterone- and Whiskey-fueled anger as men from a pub across the street come out to see what all the fuss was about.

The townspeople slowly realized what had just happened. The entire time, the fat little girl was screaming "paedo" at the top of her voice and pointing at South. The lorry driver was holding South and fending off the girl and the other bystanders, but it was clear he didn't really want to stop them from getting at South. Ellie's parents showed up and South was lucky to be escorted away by the police as quickly as he was.

The police thought it was a domestic of some sort and nearly didn't bother to handcuff South. He wasn't formally arrested at the scene. There wasn't time. He was bundled into a police car and driven away at a high speed. The police car was followed by a colorful array of unkempt vehicles.

It wasn't until they had calmed Ellie down and arrested three people for breach of the peace outside the police station that it began to become clear. They had something serious on their hands all right. At the very least, they had a man who had tried to abduct a little girl in broad daylight.

Steven South was not a dim man. He was no Einstein, but he was not stupid enough to break down and confess everything. He knew they had very little on him. He had never been arrested before. He had had a good reason to be on that road at that time of day. He said he had stopped to ask directions and had been attacked by the girl. He pleaded with the officer and asked him to pass on his sincere apologies to the girl for the obvious misunderstanding. He should not have stopped to ask directions from a young girl. He saw then that it looked bad and said he was so sorry for all of the fuss.

"What was I thinking?" he said to the police officer. "Stopping to ask directions from a schoolgirl. Of course she reacted the way she did and immediately lashed out at me. That's what we tell our kids to do. So sorry. Silly me! What a mix up."

It nearly worked, too. There were few witnesses or at least there was confusion about what they had seen and no surveillance cameras either. The girl calmed down after a while. Ellie was even encouraged by one inexperienced police officer to accept the nice man's apology and forget the whole misunderstanding. You can imagine the pressure she felt when they said that she might have overreacted a bit. She was genuinely sorry that she had broken his nose. After all, she knew that judo teachers tell you to defend, not attack. She asked if she would get in trouble.

If it had not been for the driver of the lorry, Steven South would have walked out of that police station that evening. He would have been free to continue to abduct, rape, and murder little girls. Emboldened by his brush with the law, he might have even hatched more audacious plans. But for once, luck was against him.

The driver of the lorry must have rounded the bend with seconds to spare. He must have arrived just in time to catch a glimpse of the terrified child clambering out of the white van and running for her life. He must have seen the man hold his bloodied nose and lunge to grab her back. He knew what he had seen, he knew it had not been a misunderstanding, and he wouldn't budge. The game was up.

Statements were taken. South was booked in for the night. The clock was ticking. Ellie had a nice policewomen to chat to call WPC Kennedy, and in the cold light of day on her own sofa with her mum and dad in the next room, she was not under pressure. That time, she remained quiet and calm. Her story was detailed and descriptive. She was in no doubt, and an hour later, neither was officer Kennedy.

"This is it, Sarge," Kennedy said to her sergeant. "This guy's a proper bona fide paedo. Definitely. This could be big. Trust me, Sarge, this girl's telling me the truth."

Kennedy was sure. The girl was sure, and the lorry driver was more than sure. The police got a search warrant first light the next day. A quiet, normal residential street in Liverpool was cordoned off, and the rest is history. How close they came to letting him go is frightening, but I guess now that's not relevant. They went in his house, and within ten minutes, they all started to give each other the look. The "we are on to something here" look.

Very soon they found the little girl's outfits in the wardrobe upstairs. The room had been secured well and completely remodeled inside. There were thick sheets of soundproof board on every wall, over the window, and on the inside of the door. In the room, there was only a large old hospital bed. On each side of its strong metal frame, the paint had rubbed off in a ring shape evidently by some restraints. Before long, everyone was in blue overalls, blue booties, and masks. Police photographers began to take pictures.

The word went around the force so quickly that inspector Zac Ridatt was in Liverpool before the police in Scotland had the time to bang on the cell door and shout, "We've got you now, you dirty fuckin' paedo. We've got you now." Naturally, that evening South had a very nasty fall which resulted in two broken ribs and a few stitches. South was placed on constant suicide watch. No one wanted to let him take the easy way out. Within a week he was charged and placed in a more secure facility pending trial for the attempted abduction of Ellie McLeish and the abduction and murder of Emma Forester.

CHAPTER 12

NEW YEAR'S EVE

———

2006/2007

NEW YEAR'S EVE PARTIES HAVE never been my thing—all that kissing and backslapping. I would much rather be at home with the wife and kids. But that year was different. James was going to have a party at his house. And as I had never met Laura or Jake or any of his friends and family, I was glad to accept his kind invitation. When he told me Connie had promised to come, I was beside myself.

"Seriously?" I asked.

"Yep. She is coming. She said she would, at least. I don't know why. I've invited her to all sorts of barbecues and stuff like that since we've really gotten to know each other, and I think she and Laura are good friends now. But why this New Year's Eve? I have no idea. It's a breakthrough, though, don't you think?"

I did think. It sounded like she was going to be there, and I couldn't wait to finally see her. The girl in the red cloak, although I didn't expect she would wear it to the party. I didn't know what to expect. I had built her up in my imagination so much that I almost didn't want to actually meet the real thing after all. I wondered what I would say if she spoke to me. I mean, I knew so much about her, and she didn't know I existed. I decided I would have to take care to not be too knowing or too familiar, or she would know we had been talking about her behind her back in great detail for years.

Sandi normally would take two hours to get ready for a party, but this was different. She was keener than I was to finally put some faces to names. We were both excited. The kids were happy to see in the new year in with my mum and dad and so off we went to the Foresters' house.

The party started at seven, so we got there at six forty-five. A combination of eagerness on our part, and Sandi said we may be needed to help with some preparations. In any event no one was ready for us and it was all a bit awkward. They lived in a big house on a nice street. To be honest, most streets are nice in that part of the world, and there weren't many small houses. The cars on the drives were also a bit of a giveaway.

Laura was upstairs getting dressed. She shouted some "hellos" down and demanded that Sandi go straight up to assist her with some sort of wardrobe malfunction issue. James was trying to get one of those beer keg things propped up and tapped into. He looked like a WWE wrestler in a tux. I didn't have anything remotely smart with me, so I had to make do with jeans and a jacket.

Laura had arrived on the scene at precisely seven o'clock. She had rushed down the stairs as if she had forgotten half of the preparations. In fact, though, everything was ready. All she had to do was light the candle in the huge glass dome on the front step. "There," she said. "That just sets it all off." And she finally calmed down and warmly came toward me. She was another drop-dead gorgeous creature. The place was starting to look like London Fashion Week and I looked terribly out of place, of course.

"You must be Peter, the American," she said. I said I was, even though I had been raised just down the road.

"It's so lovely to meet you," she said as she kissed me on both cheeks. "James has talked incessantly about you. I think it's a man crush."

I said something like, "The feeling is mutual," and we both laughed. She let my hand go just before it became awkward.

"Come. Come, come. Let's get Sandi and me a drink. What are you on, Peter? Beer? That won't do at all. Here. Open this."

She thrust a bottle of rosé champagne into my hand and then quickly grabbed three glasses while at the same time pouring out my beer down the sink.

"What about me?" James said as he came into the kitchen. "I see you guys have met," James said to Laura and me. I quickly introduced Sandi, and after some more air-kissing and warm smiles, we were all old friends.

"He's delightful, just as you said. We are going to have champagne. It's going to be a great year—I can feel it," Laura said. "Where are your kids, Peter? Jim, you did tell Peter to bring his wife and kids, didn't you?" She looked around the room and craned her neck to see into the living room.

"Of course I did," James said.

"Sorry, but they couldn't come," I said. "Tummy bug." That was a white lie, but Sandi thought it would be best for them to stay with Mum and Dad. In any case, they didn't want to come. You know what kids are like.

Laura was clearly determined to do more than just have a great party—she was on a mission to make changes and to live life to the fullest. Perhaps she had turned a corner. Put stuff to bed. Decided it was time. It was evident in everything she did that night, and it made for one of the best parties I had ever been to. It was a joy from its start to its finish.

Laura thrust a champagne glass toward James. "Not me," he said. "I'm on the real ale. Bit cloudy admittedly, but you know where you are with this stuff, right, Peter?"

Champagne has always given me terrible gas, but I kept that to myself, electing instead for a "champagne for me any day" frame of mind. That turned out to be a great move, as I was able to nurse the glasses for ages. People tend to top your glass up less when it's expensive champagne. When you drink beer, though, people are constantly shoving another can or bottle of beer in your hand before you've finished the first one. That's why a house is always full of half-empty beer cans at the end of a party, I reckon.

Jake was there to do the door—or at least he opened it each time the bell rang and then got people their first drinks. He looked every inch the handsome young man James had told me so much about. Sandi said he was a "dish." He wore skinny jeans and had long hair. He was like a taller, better-looking version of Mick Jagger in his twenties. I was more than a little jealous of him to be honest. I mean the swine had looks and youth.

We chatted, and he got me a beer. He seemed nice, and the conversation was easy enough. He liked to ski, and so do I. Who knows how we got on that subject, but it killed the ten minutes before he showed me his latest tattoo. It was a huge koi carp wrapped around the top of his arm and shoulder. It actually looked better than it sounds, not that I would want one or, more likely, be allowed to get one.

James joined us just as the doorbell rang out again—more neighbors, or at least I assumed they were neighbors. I decided to introduce myself later. Staying put in a corner with a clear vantage point and a close proximity to the beer fridge seemed like the best play to start with. Sadly, James had other ideas, and he beckoned me over and introduced me as a close friend from America. I felt flattered by the intro. The people all seemed nice. I was having a good time after all.

After a while spent chatting with him and then watching him with the other guests, I realized that Jake was seriously a nice guy. He's like the clichéd tall, dark, and handsome man and to top it all he is polite and not at all brash. He has perfect long dark hair. It makes you sick. I mean, how come? Lucky kid. But we got on. I forgave him for looking like the chap from the Davidoff advert. He smiled a lot even though he said very little. He had a shy, quiet air about him, but he had a smile and a sense of confidence that would always see him through. Some people are just nice to look at—sunny and perky. They don't need to try. Others could be instantly disliked for it, but not Jake. He carried it all with such a quiet humility that no one could have ever taken a disliking to him. Especially not the ladies, I fear.

One of the guests was a forty-something dentist from across the street. She was loud and drunk by eight thirty. She kept turning the music up, and I kept turning it down when she wasn't watching. Then at about ten o'clock, she caught me and roundly abused me for being gay and a square and a boring old fart. She was probably right about some of those insults, and it wasn't my house or my party, but I couldn't help myself. I was by then preoccupied with staying sober so I could watch everyone else. The last thing I wanted to do was get drunk and have my dancing shoes turn up.

I didn't want to miss a thing. I wanted to take it all in and to soak in every look or glance. I wanted to get to know the faces and the personalities I had heard so much about. I couldn't take my eyes off of James and Laura. They were so good together. One of them would lightly touch the other's forearm in passing, or they would share a quick kiss and a knowing smile that said, "It's going well."

So everything had gone great. It was about nine o'clock. Everyone was there, as far as I knew. And the food was nice. The neighbors were nice. The atmosphere was "party, party." No one seemed uneasy or awkward or difficult to talk to. I felt relaxed, and I was thinking about chatting to the chaps next to me when it happened.

Do you remember the scene in *Weird Science* when the boys are waiting for the fog to clear, and as it does their jaws fall to the floor, and time stands still as Kelly LeBrock is revealed standing in the doorway? Well, it was way more dramatic than that.

It was Connie. Every single person stopped. I swear that the music even stopped. She had on this long black P.V.C raincoat and its collar was up as high as possible. But as she took it off and handed it to Jake, she was like a butterfly emerging from its chrysalis. She wore black skintight jeans with a patent-leather stripe up the side that made her jeans look like a dinner suit. She was wrapped up tightly in a dark red men's-style shirt with a black pencil-thin neck tie. She looked like the sexiest bullfighter I had ever seen. She was ridiculously tall in blood red patent-leather heels—and her hair! It was as dark as the night and silky, curly but immaculate. It almost draped over one of her eyes like a coquettish hide-and-seek.

For someone who didn't want to be noticed, she was doing a terrible job. I am sure that the black and the coat had given her the confidence to go to the party at all. But once she arrived and discarded her coat—well, I suspect she would have felt very self-conscious if she had seen herself. Not because she looked as if she was trying too hard or because she was dressed irregularly, but because of how incredible she looked. Because of how everyone couldn't stop looking at her.

I figured that eventually she would catch sight of herself in a mirror or, more likely, that everyone looking at her would make her self-conscious. She probably wouldn't have stayed long but for one thing…Jake answered the door, you see. She nearly fell backward. She visibly swooned. They introduced themselves awkwardly with handshakes and pecks on the cheek. They did not know which side to go for, and their lips almost met. Their faces were red, and they nervously laughed. He took her coat and closed the front door. The coat missed the chair he had tried to throw it on, and neither of them watched it hit the floor. They just stood looking at each other for what seemed like way too long to the rest of us. By the way, we were all staring.

Then all at once we realized we were being voyeuristic and quickly went about our business. The music resumed. They were never seen again. I think they talked all night. No one interrupted. No one wanted to. Most of the time, she was leaning against the freezer in the garage. He was kicking a tennis ball to the dog, which gave him plenty of time to look down at his feet. We all got it immediately. Each of us oldies had had that feeling, and we gave each other a look that said, "Ah, young love." And for once, it was true, real, and inescapable. And looking back now I am proud that I was there to witness it. The moment they first met, that is.

Midnight came along on that cold British New Year's Eve and as is so awkwardly traditional, people were hugging and shaking hands.

But just out of sight—just beyond the garage doorway, tucked away where "grown-ups" couldn't see and snigger, two people were kissing like teenagers. Properly. Passionately. And for the first time in their lives.

Connie and Jake were inseparable. That winter, they spent time together at every available opportunity. It was more than just love at first sight. More than an instant infatuation. They were truly kindred spirits. Made for each other and no one else. Both tall, dark, and mysterious. Both sickeningly great-looking. Both quiet and withdrawn but easy around each other. They were like two peas in a pod. They clearly pledged their lives to each other and never looked back.

Most people spend New Year's Day on the sofa with lots of old movies and Alka-Seltzer, but not Jake and Connie. Neither one of them was much of a drinker, although Connie made an exception for good Portuguese red wine. They spent the first days of January walking along the river. They discovered that they shared a love for all things fifties, as well as for tattoos, and, unfortunately for James and Laura, body piercings. They had the same taste in music. Some awful metal noise from a band called something like System of the Down accompanied them everywhere. Naturally, the "adults" disapproved. I say "adults" because despite the fact that they were in their mid-twenties, they behaved more like love-sick teenagers.

They were constantly touching, if not kissing, in public as if they had not a care in the world for what others might have thought. And they didn't.

It was real love—real devotion. They were completely immersed in each other from the very first second they met. Connie had just started her PhD and was on the road to what we all assumed would be a remarkable career in the world of particle physics. She had already been approached by the world-famous research facility known as CERN, in Geneva.

Jake was intelligent, if not an intellectual. He was well read, if not opinionated. His would not be a life of illustrious careers, but one such player in any couple is probably enough. Jake had issues for sure. He had been immeasurably troubled by the loss of his twin sister and especially because of the circumstances surrounding her disappearance on that fateful day in June of '87. He blamed himself for not being with her on the trampoline, and he would have gladly traded places. Twins, of course, share a special bond, and Jake was naturally lost without Emma. He became a difficult child at school and being withdrawn meant friends were very few. He lumbered along alone but deliberately without causing his parents alarm. The last thing he wanted was attention or to add to his mum and dad's distress. So he lived with it all buried as deep as he could. His grades suffered and he came to rely on his mother more and more for emotional support and eventually a roof over his head. If he had not met Connie, things for him would have been very different indeed.

Jake and Connie had much in common. They were both quiet and studious. Interested, but not overly inquisitive. At any rate, they were not the type to pry or gossip. They got the questions about each other's past out of the way early. Connie didn't go into too much detail about her past. She shed enough light on her previous life to illuminate it sufficiently, but no more than that. Jake talked at length about Emma and how the situation had shaped the man he had become. Connie never once let on that she knew all about his twin sister from her long conversations with his father. It didn't seem appropriate or necessary to bring Jake into her entire past world. She touched on the car journeys with James. Jake knew most of it from listening in to the conversations his mother and father had shared each evening back then, but he politely pretended to Connie that it was all news to him.

At any rate, it was sort of all in the past for both of them. Connie especially had moved on significantly since meeting James. And Jake took her to another level. Everyone enjoyed their company, and Connie became even more comfortable at the Foresters' house, where many a pleasant Sunday roast was prepared.

CHAPTER 13

TRIAL

———

Christmas 2006.

IT WAS THE END OF another Christmas break, the
second in a row in which I had spent almost every
evening with my newfound friend, James Forester.
But now it was time for me, Sandi, and the girls to
head back to America. Fay and Jaz were about sixteen
and fourteen respectively, and although they had enjoyed spending so much time with their grandparents,
they were naturally very excited to be getting home to
their school friends.

I had enjoyed my evenings with James. I had been
rocked by the story that had unfolded over the past
few evenings, but like the last year, 1 couldn't wait to
get home to research all of the people and events in
more detail. I wanted to know it all. I was obsessed for
sure. I had a morbid fascination with some of the players in the story. Sandi was getting increasingly drawn

in, too. She was as voracious as I was when it came to the research, and every detail we discovered about South and the Liverpool house sent shivers down our spines.

Thanks to the Internet, which was full of newspaper articles from the time, e-mails from James, and the fantastic public records system, which the UK courts had made available online, we were all over the details of the trial and we read every scrap about it from start to finish.

As planned, the trial of one Steven Andrew South had taken place nine months later that year. A jury of twelve impartial men and women must have been hard to find thanks to the constant press coverage. But a jury was indeed sworn in on November 1, 2002, and the trial began. James and Laura made the trip to the world-famous London court, "The Old Bailey," most days. God knows how they found the strength to drive there and back daily and to sit within twenty feet of the monster who had taken their daughter.

As predicted, South continued to smile at the gallery and offered no comments. He denied having anything to do with any of it and said instead that he would let friends use his house when he was away. He pleaded not guilty to all of the charges, including to the charge of making and distributing indecent images of children. He also pleaded not guilty to the abduction, false imprisonment, rape, and murder of

Emma Forester in June 1987. He said he hadn't been in town.

Then there was the abduction, false imprisonment, rape, and murder of one Libby Dengelo, who, it turned out, was the little black seven-year-old. (She had not been reported missing until years later because of her parents' dodgy immigration status.) South told the court he had paid an unknown man cash to pave his lawn while he was away for a few weeks and that he had no knowledge of the girl buried under it. Lastly, there was the attempted abduction of Ellie McLeish in broad daylight. To that charge, he said he had simply pulled over to ask directions and was attacked by the little girl.

He would go on to blame others. To deny any knowledge of what had happened. To claim to have been away at the time. To have never met the girls.

The prosecution was a strange-looking bunch. One of them was a ridiculously tall black female barrister named Penelope Stansell, and the other two were fat young men. Luckily for them, she did all of the standing. They seemed to be there to slide Ms. Stansell slips of paper from time to time.

To say the prosecution barristers were out of their depth would be an understatement. From the beginning, James had had serious and well-founded concerns that South would walk. South, of course, had legal aid, and back in those days, that meant a top defense lawyer for free. Each firm of barristers had to offer up their time to represent clients on behalf of the legal aid system. It was a system designed to ensure a fair trial. In effect, it meant that scumbags got the best lawyers in the land at the taxpayers' expense. In the United States, we have a similar system called "pro bono."

Back in England the best of the best in the legal profession make it to the rank of Q.C.—that's Queen's Counsel to you and me—which means they represent the crown and they get the right to dress up in the traditional gown and silk wig. Hence the nickname "silk."

On that occasion, the random selection system had offered up one of the brightest Queen's Counsel in England. He was a world-renowned silk called Richard M. Taylor-Smithe. The Scottish truck driver who was to be the prosecution's star witness was sadly killed just weeks before the trial began in a terrifying plunge from a mountain road near Chamonix, France. To make matters worse, he had been drinking and so his evidence, given to the court in the form of his original police statement, was naturally tainted.

Nevertheless, it was compelling to hear his police statement from beyond the grave, so to speak, and he was pretty clear that what he had seen had been nothing short of an abduction. Taylor-Smithe argued compellingly to the contrary and attempted to have his statement stricken from the record because he was a known drinker and was not available for a cross-examination. Luckily for the prosecution, his request was denied by the judge.

The key evidence in the attempted abduction case was, of course, Ellie McLeish. She was a larger-than-life girl who turned thirteen on the second day of the trial and was granted her wish to appear in person at the Old Bailey. Although she remained behind a screen, she refused anonymity and often appeared in the Scottish press soon after the trial ended. She became somewhat of a minor celebrity in Glasgow. She championed self-defense and was soon the podgy poster girl for a chain of judo classes.

After such a harrowing experience, a normal girl that age would have taken the opportunity to give evidence via a video filmed in her hometown. But not Ellie. As South had found out that fateful day, she was made of sterner stuff. Ellie was cross-examined by Taylor-Smithe. He was gentle at first. But when she refused to budge, the tall, gruff silk became too energetic for the judge. The no-nonsense Senior Lord Justice Wakefield had more trials under his belt than all of the prosecution and defense barristers combined. He had been in the big chair for a number of high-profile child sexual abuse cases. He knew how to handle the barristers and, more importantly, how to protect the children from overenthusiastic cross-examinations.

In any event Little Ellie explained herself vociferously,

"He grabbed me from under the van where I was hiding from him, and he chucked me in the side door. I kicked at him as hard as I could, 'cause I knew I was done for otherwise. He got it in the face. I was out of there in a flash, I was."

"Did he say anything to you?" Ms. Stansell asked.

"No, nothing at all."

"Did he ask you directions?"

"To whereabouts?" Ellie replied.

"Anywhere at all. Did he ask you for directions to anywhere at all? Was he lost, and is that why he talked to you?"

"No. No, he never said a word. He just grabbed me, and it was as quick as that. He grabbed me. He bruised me. You've seen the pictures just now. Guy's a paedo. Grabbed me, and I was done for. End of story."

Lord Justice Wakefield didn't care for the wording, but it had been said, and he just glared at the prosecution's desk. They knew what he meant, but how can you stop a youngster from using youngster language?

Mr. South had over nine hundred indecent images of children on his computer. There were also the little girls' clothes that had been found in his house. The DNA of at least six different girls had been discovered on those precious little garments and elsewhere in his house. Eventually three other victims would be identified by the forensic examiners thanks to DNA evidence and advances in technology. Three more families would receive that knock on their doors. The news they had both dreaded and dreamed of. The fates of their loved ones had been revealed. The face of the monster had been illuminated.

South said nothing whenever possible. He refused to admit to anything, and more importantly, he refused to say where Emma or the others were.

Luckily the prosecution barrister, Ms. Stansell, was much better at her job than the press said she appeared. Tall and scruffy, she certainly made her mark in the room. She towered menacingly over the rest of the court as she started on South.

"We know Emma was in that room. We know for a fact that she was there for years. You abducted her. We know that you were working not far from her house the day she disappeared. We can prove you were there. We can prove she was in your house. Why don't you just save us all a lot of time? Why don't you do the decent thing and tell this poor family what you did with their beautiful little girl?"

He did not comment. As usual, he just smiled and shrugged his shoulders.

Ms. Stansell continued now more ferociously. "We know you had others. We will find their names and their families. We will find the mothers and fathers whose lives you have destroyed for your own sick sexual gratification. We will prove that you killed and buried little Libby Dengelo. There was no patio man, was there?"

"Don't Remember," South replied.

"You must recall his name. If I gave someone a job to do at my house, I would recall the man's name. Did he give you a receipt?"

But again no meaningful reply from South.

"We will prove that you converted that room in your house into a dungeon. We will show that it was you who purchased the materials from a local builders' merchant. We know it was you who held young girls captive in that room for considerable periods of time. Why don't you just admit what you did to those poor girls?"

"Don't remember do I," he said with a bigger smile. But those simple words were more damning than he anticipated.

Perhaps he was pleased that they knew that there had been more than one or two girls. Perhaps he was proud of himself. He certainly came across like he felt a sense of achievement. Thankfully, the jury noticed it too.

"You travel quite a lot, don't you, Mr. South?"

"I suppose."

"To Bangkok. Is that correct?"

"So what?"

"Is that a 'yes'?"

"Yes, so what? Lots of people go there on holiday."

"What is it about Bangkok that you find so fascinating?"

"Piss off!"

"Order!" the judge said. "Any more of that language and I will hold you in contempt of court."

"I know what you are trying to suggest," South sneered.

"Why are you getting so angry, Mr. South? What am I trying to suggest? Is it because you're aware that Bangkok is known as the most desirable destination for paedophiles?"

"Not why I went there!" South said in a slow deliberate voice.

"Steven, can I call you Steven? Are you a paedophile Steven?"

"No, you cannot, and no, I am not," said South.

"Why Bangkok then?" Stansell probed. "Twice a year for as far back as we can go. Why? Why did you regularly visit Bangkok? Why was your blood found in the hedge in Emma Forester's back garden? You're a murderer and a child killer and a disgusting paedophile, aren't you?"

"Fuck you, bitch," South shouted with spit flying from his mouth.

"Order. Order." Lord Justice Wakefield was about to hold South in contempt of court for what would be the first of many times during the trial. Proceedings were halted and South was awarded a twenty-day prison sentence for his outbursts to be served either after his acquittal or on top of any conviction sentence.

When things resumed an hour or so later, Ms. Stansell continued.

"You had an Internet business, didn't you, Mr. South?"

That shocked South as much as the blood evidence had. He thought of the scratched arms he had gotten when he had snatched Emma all of those years ago. He was getting hot. His face was considerably redder. He knew what was on the computer and that it was only a matter of time.

"You made a healthy living from an Internet business, didn't you? Mr. South?"

"Not really, so what?"

"What did you provide in return for the subscription, then? I mean, it cost a great deal of money, didn't it? What did people get for their thirty pounds a month? It must have been good. Thirty pounds a month, and hundreds of people subscribed, didn't they?"

"Yes. It was all legit. It was a web design and hosting business. I paid my taxes and everything."

"Only it wasn't a hosting business, was it? It was pictures of young girls, wasn't it?"

"No."

"Yes. Yes, it was, and we have your computer. We have evidence that will prove that you filmed girls as young as six or seven years old. You made them do things to each other on camera. You regularly promised young girls money or cigarettes, alcohol and even drugs so they would perform for you, didn't you? Did you or did you not offer to sell one of the girls live on air? You called the auction 'Teenbay,' didn't you? Why are you looking to the gallery, Mr. South? Is there someone there who you think can help you? Don't worry—we will find your accomplices, too."

Then South was really squirming. He knew that they didn't just have him but that they also had information about hundreds of other men like him. He knew that the knock on the door was close for them, too.

"During the time you held poor Emma captive in your homemade dungeon, you visited Thailand eleven times. On one occasion, you stayed there for exactly thirty-seven days, did you not?"

"I don't know any Emma girl, and so what if I did go to Thailand? If I did go, it was for a few days."

"Mr. South, these are the facts. The undeniable truth is here before the court. Your passport is stamped. The airline confirmed your seats. The credit card bills don't lie like you do. Are you saying those are all wrong?"

"No."

"So they are right?"

"I guess."

"You guess. Well, you guess correctly. You were there."

"If you say so."

"I do say so, because it is undeniably the truth. I put it to you that you chained poor Emma to the bed while you were away sunning yourself in Bangkok. Isn't that true, Mr. South?

"No," he shouted.

"You left her with nothing to eat or drink for thirty-seven days while you were feasting on young girls."

"No."

"You killed her."

"No."

"You might as well have put a gun to her head and pulled the trigger. You murdered Emma Forester, didn't you? You abducted her, you raped her, and when she was too old to fulfill your sick obsession with very young girls, you murdered her, didn't you?"

"No," he said quietly now as his head started to drop. His smile was long gone.

CHAPTER 14

JUSTICE

———

T HE TRIAL CONTINUED FOR FIVE more weeks. South gradually broke. He knew the game was up for him. The computer evidence proved that he had abducted, groomed, abused, filmed, and exploited very young girls. The forensic evidence at the Liverpool house proved that there had been at least three long-term residents in the dungeon and countless visitors to the various mattresses.

After the video evidence was presented, many young local girls came forward to the police or social services. They were mostly reluctant to talk about what had happened to them in great detail. But the huge scale of South's operation was becoming clear for all to see. Following the Steven South conviction, the paedophile ring he had run was smashed wide open, and dozens of men eventually went to jail.

In the end, no fancy "silk" could explain away the mountain of evidence against him. Taylor-Smithe,

QC, was handed a very rare loss in his otherwise illustrious career. But it wasn't luck that had shut the cell door on South for the rest of his life.

Ms. Penelope Stansell had done a fine job, and it's no surprise that she got QC silk soon after. Mark Benson, who had led the original search for Emma, and his replacement, Inspector Ridatt, sat with Laura and James on the old brown leather benches just outside of courtroom number one. They drank tea and said little as they waited before being given the signal by the clerk of the court to return to their seats inside. The jury filed in, having deliberated for just two and a half hours before returning a unanimous guilty verdict on all charges.

Lord Justice Wakefield held nothing back in his sentencing of South some eight weeks later in the spring of 2003. Everyone including the world's press returned to court to hear the judge send him down with these words.

"You are a predator. A dangerous and depraved individual who has shown no remorse for your heinous crimes. The lives you have destroyed can never be mended. The lives you have taken can never be replaced. I have no doubt that you would have continued to murder if you had not been caught. I therefore have no choice but to impose the maximum sentence available. Life in prison. Take him down."

Suffice it to say, South knew then that he would never see the light of day again.

As he was being taken away by at first one and then three officers of the court, he passed within three feet of James and Laura. South couldn't help but give the Forester family one last torturous twist of the knife.

After stopping and laughing, he shouted, "I only like the fresh meat, I fucking killed her when her little pussy started to smell." South theatrically sniffed the air In front of Laura and said, "Like yours, you old slag."

James dived over the railings in a fist-first lunge, but he was restrained by Ridatt just before he got himself locked up as well.

As South was dragged away by the reinforcements, he kicked his legs out against the walls of the stairs leading down and shouted, "I know where I dumped the little bitch, you know. I might tell you one day."

And just as they rounded the corner at the foot of the stairs, the officers closest to him heard him shout, "I'll tell if you visit me, Laura."

Of course, as the months went by, Laura considered visiting South. We all strongly advised her against it. After all, he was never going to tell her where he had buried Emma. Why would he? If Laura had visited, he would have said, "I will tell you next time," to keep her coming back. He would have enjoyed the limited power and influence it would briefly give him. It's quite a common tactic when faced with life behind bars. It's about the only way to get attention. Brady and Hindley, the notorious child killers who buried their five little victims' bodies in shallow graves on Saddleworth Moor, had done that sort of thing for years in the sixties. As with them, it would have meant an endless stream of visits for South from relatives of the deceased or from writers and journalists. Each visitor hoping that he would tell. But he never would. Brady even got visits out to the moors. Those visits were like a jolly day-trip for him. We will never know if he ever intended to take searchers to the correct spot. I doubt it. They never found the bodies, but Brady got out of his cell for the day each time.

One morning in August of 2003, James got a call from the prison. He answered, and they wanted to check that Laura was all right. They wanted to be sure that no harm had come to her on the way to the prison because she had never arrived. James was naturally very worried because Laura hadn't told him anything about an intended visit to the prison. He was also quite angry at the thought of her seeing South at all. They had talked about it once, but they both agreed it was out of the question.

When Laura got home, James was understandably a little angry and upset, but she just laughed. It was the first time she had laughed like that in what must have seemed like years. She was filled with a really childish joy. James didn't see the funny side of it at all until she explained.

She'd just gone for a walk. A long walk, and she sat on the riverbank and smiled. And then she laughed, and she couldn't stop. You see Laura had written to the prison and arranged to visit South that day, but of course she never intended to go. She just sat there on a park bench thinking of him all dressed up and eager to torment her, and she didn't show. I bet he was furious and that the guards took the piss.

It was more than a little childish, but Laura deserved it, I guess. Anyway, that was the last of that "to visit or not" debate except that Laura did it to him again a few months later.

Laura and James were the subject of much public interest, of course. They decided it would be best not to try to hide away. Instead, they put their efforts into helping the other families and the other victims. They thought that they might uncover fresh leads along the way or that they would discover Emma's whereabouts perhaps. Maybe others would even be brought to justice.

James went back to work soon after the trial ended, and then there was the cancer and Connie. Starting to talk about it all, which dragged it all back up again. But for Laura, it never left. Then one bright sunny day in October of 2003 and only a few weeks after

Laura's last prank prison visit, there was a sharp knock at their door. It was not one but two uniformed police officers this time. South was dead.

It would be the subject of an internal prison investigation, but it appeared as though South had been assaulted with a pool cue on one of the prison landings. His credentials had been leaked to some of the other lifers who had young kids of their own. The pool cue had been inserted into South's backside while he was held down. After a few good stout kicks to the fat end of the cue stick, the tip eventually exited through his neck. He screamed like a newborn baby and bled to death in fifteen agonizing minutes. By all accounts the fellow prisoners formed a human barrier, deliberately preventing medical attention and prolonging South's' inevitable demise.

Laura and James said nothing. They did not know how to feel. It was a shame that he wouldn't rot in jail for many decades to come, but it was a fine ending indeed. They realized that any chance of finding Emma had probably died with South. That was the hardest part to cope with. But every time they thought of him in agony, it helped tremendously.

CHAPTER 15

YARD

———

October 2004.

J AMES FORESTER WAS DIAGNOSED WITH testicular can-cer on the seventh of January 2004. That very day he met and befriended the young, beautiful, strange but alluring Connie Blake.

His car broke down in early May propelling Laura into the mix. In June James had surgery to remove the offending article and he reluctantly followed that in July with a course of chemotherapy. So he had already had a busy year when out of the blue in October, he discovered something which shook him to his core.

"James, it's Mark on the phone," Laura said quietly.

"Mark who, babe?"

"Benson," she replied louder.

James said, "Really? OK," as he tentatively took the phone from Laura's outstretched hand, giving her a quizzical look that said, what's this going to be about?

"Hi, Mark, it's Jim. What's up?"

"Jim, nice to speak, family OK?" former inspector Benson began.

"You know Ridatt has still not given up, don't you, Jim? I mean, he's never going to close the case until he finds every bastard on every computer file, or whatever."

"I know, Mark. Laura and I will always be glad for everything you all have done for us and for our Emma."

Mark assured James that absolutely no gratitude was necessary and then continued, "Well, Ridatt wants to meet. To debrief, or whatever. Knock heads together, that sort of thing. He has asked me to be there and wondered if you would come, too. What do you say James?"

"Of course, but I'm not sure what—" James tried to say.

"Just come, mate. We never know, do we?" Mark butted in.

"OK, sure," James said. "Of course, if you think so. When?"

————

It was only a short walk from the Saint James Park tube station to Victoria Street. Then there it was. He was going inside New Scotland Yard. Him. A teacher. Bloody hell, he thought. Cool. Then he remembered why.

"Jim!" Mark was there at the door to meet him, which was a relief.

"You good to go?"

"Ready as I will ever be," Jim said. "Although I have no idea what good any of this will do. We have been over it all a thousand times in the past eighteen years."

Still, there James was, surrounded by big glass walls, shiny stone floors, and top-ranking uniforms. He was smack in the center of Westminster and a stone's throw from Buckingham Palace. It was quite exciting, and deep down, he was delighted that Emma's file was still well and truly open. They were booked in and given hot laminated passes to be worn around their necks at all times.

Then as if he still worked there, Mark led James to a lift in the corner of the lobby and up to a huge open room of working policemen and women. Every one of them was busy catching baddies, he thought. It was a good start.

Isaac Ridatt, or rather Chief Inspector Ridatt, as he by then was, met them at the door to his glass box of an office. While they greeted each other, his assistant took their orders for tea and coffee, and James had a chance to glance around. Then just as quickly he wondered if he was supposed to be looking around at all the police work on the walls. What if he had seen something confidential or something that had to do with an ongoing case? The walls were plastered in scraps of paper, and on the glass, there was a series of red lines joining one scumbag to another—or one den of iniquity to a scumbag, and one scumbag to a massive seizure of drugs. Thankfully, he didn't recognize anyone.

They had their tea and coffee while Mark and Zac caught up with the case. James listened intently, but there didn't seem to be any new developments. The house in Liverpool had been taken apart, put back together, sold, and demolished, and a new house was currently being built on the site by a local property developer who Ridatt said was a former Liverpool football player. A mental picture of Fred West's house on Cromwell Street flashed in front of James's eyes, and he imagined someone new living there now. The notorious child killer had buried his victims in the cellar and even bricked some of them into the walls. Good luck selling the new house in Liverpool, he thought.

The conversation turned to a list of people who had been interviewed, including some who had been identified as men who had worked on the Internet porn with South.

The tone hushed a bit at that point, and the others tried to move on out of respect for James. He knew what they were alluding to and trying to protect him from. The Internet videos. Emma. The stuff she had been forced to do on camera.

Laura and James had already talked it through with Ridatt and had decided they couldn't watch. They wanted it all destroyed but understood that it had to be kept as evidence. Because everything had been encrypted and sent through foreign Internet service providers, it took a very long time to get hold of. By that time, South was dead. And they didn't want to see it. Or couldn't bear to see it. Even though it would have been a chance to see Emma all grown up. It was a tough decision, but who would really want to see his or her daughter in that way? They couldn't, and James had a bad enough time imagining it every time Zac mentioned the Internet.

In total, over two hundred people were arrested for watching the content of South's Internet business. The computers gave up each and every one eventually. James had had no idea that there were that many perverts walking around. Then there was the list of names, none of which meant anything to him. They had interviewed them all in the hope that one of them knew something about Emma or about any of the other girls. They were all just perverts with no connections to South beyond their sick taste for young girls and boys.

"What about the boat?" James suddenly said, trying to change the subject.

"What boat, Jim?" Mark asked. But he quickly realized which boat James had meant. "The Marlow boat, you mean?"

"Yes," James said. "What about the Marlow boat? Have you still got it? I mean, there have been advances in DNA and all that. I know we got South, but what if there were others? Other men, I mean. Involved. Or other girls. Using the same boat, I mean." James was getting quite excited, but the others made it clear it was a dead end.

Mark said quickly, "I don't think we ever had it Jim. It belonged to a local chap. The guy was away, and South decorated his boathouse or something. Stayed there a couple of days and used the chap's boat without his knowledge to…well, you know."

"Take Emma," James said, which made them all look down at the floor for a few seconds.

"I don't think South and this boat owner chap were connected. I don't know much about this. It was before my time," Zac said.

"He was away! He had nothing to do with it," Mark said a little too sternly. "I mean, I recall. Didn't he say he hardly met the guy? And South was long gone when they returned from their holiday. They never even paid him. South gave a false name—or we presumed he had when it turned out that no one of that name existed, anyway the trail vanished there and then.

Mark continued more matter-of-factly now as he flicked through a thick Yellow file, "South said his name was John Jones. Worked in Marlow just two or three days. Didn't even finish the job, and then he disappeared. It was this chap—what's his name—who called the police because his boat had been used and because South had only done half the job and then left in a hurry. We checked the guy out at the time, Jim. Nothing doing there. Respected businessman. A high-flying lawyer or something. We know South used the boat to take Emma, Jim. But what good does that do us? It was just opportunity knocking. South was out enjoying himself on someone else's boat while the owner was out of the country. Then South saw the lane that runs from the river, and he thought, 'Why not?' He might have even heard the kids playing in the garden from the river. It's not far up the lane from the riverbank. He couldn't help himself. It was over in seconds, and the next day, the bastard was back in Liverpool. I have a picture of the boat here somewhere"—Mark said as he rummaged through file after file—"Here you go. Nice boat. Old style. Sorry," he quickly added when he realized how tactless that was.

"There are three or four of these here from all sorts of angles," Mark continued. "They're a bit washed out by now, I'm afraid. Take one if you'd like, Jim."

"Thanks," James said. He didn't want the picture, but he took it anyway. Mark wanted him to feel involved and in the loop, so he took the picture and studied it as if he was an expert. "Yep, that's a boat all right, detectives," James joked as he forced himself to make light of the situation, but what little laughter this provoked was soon completely blown away when James heard Mark say—

"Blake."

"Sorry, what did you say?" James asked as his grin went away.

"Blake. His name was Alan Blake," Mark said again.

"Whose name was?" James was trying to stay calm.

"The guy who owned the boat. Alan Blake. It says it here. He had bought the house in Marlow six months before, and the boat had come with it."

"Banker," Zac said as if it were a swear word.

"That's right," Mark said as he pointed his finger at Zac. "Fucking rich city banker. It was the wife who was the lawyer. Nice couple, actually. The commander went with me to speak to them personally. He knew her from somewhere, I think. You know? The wife, that is."

James had glazed over, but he remembered them explaining why they were all so sure that the Blakes hadn't known the guy. They explained how South had got the keys for the boat because he needed to move it when he painted the boathouse and how shocked the Blakes were to discover he had slept in it and used it to take Emma. How appalled they were, and how it was kept out of the press because she was in an embarrassingly high political office and there was no need to make waves.

James was desperately trying to keep it together. He had no idea why he didn't say that he knew of the guy straight away. He couldn't compute what to do with this new information fast enough. What it meant to him, to Connie. To the police. So he just sat on his hands, the color draining from his face. He really thought he would faint if he didn't get out of there.

"Are you OK, Jim?" Mark asked.

"Actually, I feel a bit hot. I think I need some air," James stuttered.

So Mark quickly wound up the day with, "Well, if we are all done for a bit, shall we leave it at that then? Zac? Jim?"

"Yep, great. Thanks." And James was out and in the taxi as quickly as possible.

He felt as if he had been holding his breath from when the word "Blake" had been uttered to when the taxi pulled away from Scotland Yard. He breathed in huge gulps of air and pulled the picture out from his jacket pocket.

As they rounded the corner, the driver said, "Where to?"

"Paddington Station," James said without looking up. And then quieter still, he said, "Home."

CHAPTER 16

CONNIE

———

"BY THE TIME I GOT to know Connie's story, we had been sharing a car for over a year. By that time, we felt comfortable talking openly with each other about our respective ills. She was always more guarded than I was, but then she was more guarded than anyone I had ever met.

"My ills were well understood by then, and my treatment for testicular cancer had gone better than I had expected it to. It was tough, sure, but thousands have done it, and I just had to get it done. I am one of the lucky ones because it stopped the cancer from spreading, at least for the time being. I would be able to look forward to a couple of years– or maybe much more. It helped me tremendously to have some perspective put back in my life, and I grasped it with both hands. What Connie told me had changed me forever. From that day forward, I refused to feel any self-pity. I refused to look back or to say 'why me?'

"Connie, on the other hand, was almost beyond help. She never wanted pity, but she was helpless and pitiful nonetheless. Every time I saw her, I just wanted to give her a big hug. But that was the last thing anyone should have ever done to Connie. She recoiled when anyone got near her. I was like a safety screen at times. I would make excuses for her when we were together and an introduction was required. I am not sure that was the right thing to do, and no one asked me to do it, but I did it anyway. For instance when the dean stopped me at the gate to ask me a question and he leant in the car window to talk. I tried to say something like, 'Tony, this is Connie. Connie, this is Tony,' but you can imagine how awkward it was when Connie just nodded her head about a half-inch dead ahead.

"After some time together she told me about the man in Portugal. She had thought of him as a father figure, but he was very old. He had been very stern, and she hadn't even known his name. He had never allowed her out of the house, and her only memories of those early years were of servitude. I can't imagine how hard it must have been for her to be just four or five years old and nothing but a servant.

"She told me one morning that she had no idea what a mum and dad are. She had no way of computing what the word 'parent' means to a child—no point of reference at all. As far as Connie was concerned she didn't ever have parents and had never been treated as a daughter by anyone ever. Her early life had been filled with cooking and cleaning from morning to late at night. Her only savior had been the small, dilapidated farmhouse full of books.

"Connie told me about the first time she read a proper book, I think it was *Treasure Island* or something like that, and how from that moment on, she was hooked. She would read anything and everything whenever she could, even through the night. At the time, it was a tough life, she only went to school two afternoons a week when the old man went to the market which was the only time he would permit her to leave the farmhouse, but she had the books, so it hadn't seemed so bad. She recalled it with some fondness, especially when she compared it to what happened next.

"One Monday morning as I drove, Connie told me with tears running down her face about the afternoon when a man came to the farm to buy something. She was to sit in the kitchen with them while the deal was done. She remembered that the man had also been Portuguese and that he had on thick glasses. He was much younger than the old man and was clearly in charge of the negotiations.

"The stranger across the table looked her up and down as he talked. She had seen that done many times before with chickens or pigs when the bargaining had gotten heated and had gone on for ages.

"She would usually be washing dishes or the kitchen floor, but that time Connie was allowed to just sit there. It was a much-needed break from the chores she must have thought. 'She remembered swinging her legs as she sat on the kitchen chair and feeling happy to be doing nothing at all except swinging her legs.

"After what seemed to her like ages, the stranger slammed down his cup, and his chair moved back suddenly with a loud squeal on the slate floor. Both men leapt to their feet, and she thought there was going to be trouble. But thankfully, they quickly smiled and shook hands as they turned to warmly look at her.

"'You're going on an adventure. Pack some things,' the old man had said. And the deal was done.

"Connie said that she couldn't recall ever going further than the market square, which was itself only about a mile from her house. The market was full of noise and animals and going there was the highlight of her week. So it certainly must have been exciting to be in a car for the very first time. After a few days, though, she was very frightened.

"She remembered that the nights got colder and colder as they drove on. They slept in the car, and the man cuddled her tightly 'to keep warm', he said.

"'I remember snippets of a long car journey,' Connie said. 'I will never forget the smell of the blankets he made me hide under from time to time.'

"She must have been such a young, petrified little thing. It broke my heart to imagine it.

"We were driving in light snow last winter when Connie said, 'Do you remember the first time you ever saw snow?' She said she had woken up in the middle of the night still wrapped in the smelly blankets, but not in a car. She was in a cold, strange dark room. She had tiptoed to the window to look out at the fishing boats as she had done for as long as she could remember. But the boats were not there. The ocean was not there. Instead the ground was white for as far as the eye could see.

"'The strangest sight I had ever seen,' Connie said. "The cold rose up through her legs, and the glass began to fog over from her breath." Those were new, strange sensations for Connie, and at that moment she realized she was not at the farm by the beach. She was far, far from home.

"Connie told me that she just stood there for ages, looking out at the strange new landscape and crying. She was so frightened that she didn't know what to do.' Where could she have run? Out into the cold? Who could she have screamed for?

"I think most people would have missed their mum, but Connie no longer had one to miss. What could take the place of a mother? Just fear, I guess.

"Now as you well know I had been accustomed to Connie saying ten words a day until then, so I was pleasantly surprised when she continued.

"In the morning, someone just kicked her. Kicked her really hard and then pushed her from the warm bed onto the cold hard floor.

"Connie had cried out and begged for it to stop or to know what she had done, but the woman towering over her had no intention of stopping. When kicking Connie failed to have the desired effect, which must have been to make her get up, she was dragged to her feet by her ear. The strange woman called out for a man to come in. Then the two of them inspected Connie for some time like it was the normal thing to do.

"Connie told me that the couple looked her up and down, prodded her, poked her, spun her 'round, and pulled down her knickers. She was inspected in every way imaginable as if she were a prize bull at the county show.

"'I didn't understand the language they were speaking,' Connie said. 'In fact, I didn't know that there were different languages in the world. I didn't know there was a world. So I didn't protest. I just did as I was told. I thought that what they were doing might well have been normal. If I had only known how lucky I had been to be an old man's slave in Portugal, I never would have gotten in that car. They would have had to kill me first. I have wished I was dead many times since.'"

"Though Connie had no idea who these two were at the time she eventually knew them to be Mr. and

Mrs. Jan and Robert Simms, a dysfunctional couple from a dilapidated house in the back end of the Kent countryside. The Simms pair managed to convince everyone for years that Connie was a distant relative who had been sent to the UK to live with them until her parents could get the money and papers needed to join her. It transpired eventually that they had actually paid our bespectacled Portuguese friend £4500 for Connie to do with as they pleased. And what pleased Jan and Robert Simms more than anything was sexual depravity with children.

"As we drove our usual route together, over the next few weeks, she would talk in small bursts or almost outbursts about what had happened to her in the few years she had spent at the mercy of those two perverted, evil scumbags. I was spared few details. During her first day in England, she was vigorously bathed by the strange man and then immediately sexually assaulted by the woman. The man was permitted to watch, and the woman said that if he was 'a good little boy' he would be allowed to touch Connie's genitals.

"'I had absolutely no idea what was going on,' she said. 'I was only about seven at the time, and until he made me shower with him, I hadn't even seen a picture of a man's parts.' Within a few weeks Connie was being regularly sexually assaulted by both of them. I can't even bring myself to tell you the things she said they did to her.

"It wasn't surprising then that Connie couldn't wait to get to school each day and she used hard study as a way to shut off parts of her mind, parts of herself.

"In addition to learning English quickly and speaking it better than most of the other kids, she also perfected the art of hiding what was going on at home. Her skill of making herself invisible was already being honed. The only thing she looked forward to was school, and she would have gladly gone there all summer if she could have.

"In the evenings, she was the last to leave for home, and she would always arrive an hour early the next day. It's true that she would have done anything to get away from home, but it was more than that—she discovered that she was a gifted and natural intellect who genuinely enjoyed school and found learning fun.

"One evening as we drove home from Oxford, I recall Connie saying, 'I don't know who I got it from, of course, but I just found it easy and couldn't see why others in my class didn't.'

"While she excelled away from home, the time she spent there was filled with verbal and sexual abuse, and it wasn't long before one or two teachers started to ask questions.

"They wondered about the marks on her arms and why she had 'fallen down the stairs' so many times. Social workers visited the house at least ten times before anyone noticed that there was something wrong.

It was thanks to a vigilant teacher at school that eventually someone grasped the seriousness of it all and intervened.

"One afternoon when Connie reluctantly returned home she was met by a female police officer. The constant pressure exerted by the school had paid off. The police didn't need much more than the collection of child pornography found on the Simms' computer to convict them of serious offences. Turning up unannounced with a search warrant was all it took in the end and Connie was free. Mr. and Mrs. Simms on the other hand are still thankfully in prison to this day. One can only hope that the rumors are true about the treatment of child abusers who find themselves behind bars.

"At the tender age of ten years old, Connie was spared the indignity of having to testify at a trial. Her statement together with the medical examiners' reports and hundreds of nasty home videos in which Mr. and Mrs. Simms starred alongside children and animals were all enough to force the dreaded couple to plead guilty to all the charges.

"Connie was placed in foster care for a brief but blissful time while her nationality and status were confirmed. The UK authorities could not find any living relatives even with the help of the border agencies, consulate, and the Portuguese embassy, and so she was made a ward of the state. They thought that if she was given citizenship and a loving family, perhaps she could be mended after all. Maybe that is exactly what would have become of her if the Blakes had not been trying to adopt a child at that time."

CHAPTER 17

BLAKES

———

James to Peter, Christmas 2006.

"CONSTANCIA MARIA COSTA-SANTOS DE ALAMEDA'S birth certificate and school uniform were collected from the Simms's house. She didn't even have enough possessions to fill one suitcase. Connie was born on the nineteenth of April 1982 in Estoril, Portugal. Her mother was deceased, and her father was unknown. She had been beaten, abused, and made to endure unspeakable cruelty before she was eleven years old.

"Can you imagine what it must have been like to be her? To have been damaged by everyone who was ever supposed to care for her?

"What a relief it must have been—what an unbelievable slice of good fortune it must have seemed— to be driven in a huge posh car up a long manicured drive to a lavish and beautiful old house. Imagine the joy she must have felt to be under warm clean sheets in a safe and wonderful place for the very first time in her life.

"And so it was for quite some time. Mr. and Mrs. Blake were thirty-something professionals from London. At the time, Alan Blake was a city banker. That actually meant something back then. To be precise, he was a very senior director of one of the oldest and now most infamous banking institutions in the world, the Barings Bank. The bank was worth billions when Alan took his early retirement in 1994. Just one year later, it was bankrupted by a rogue trader in Singapore and sold for one pound to the ING Group. He had gotten out just in time!

"By all accounts, Alan Blake walked away with about seventy million pounds, which was quite a lot in ninety-four! He had always been a highflier, but when he retired he was super wealthy, respected, and very well connected. Having enjoyed a short but successful career in the city, it was time to devote himself to his new family and his old friends, who were in very high places.

"Hillary Blake was the same age and no less impressive. She had shone at the all-girls school in Wiltshire where she had earned top grades and a place at Cambridge University. There, she dazzled Alan and everyone else, and she was assured that she would have a successful career in whatever field she chose. First she chose law, and then politics. She eventually became one of the few aides to Prime Minister John Major shortly after he was thrust into power following Thatcher's resignation in November 1990.

"She worked behind the scenes as an influential figure in British politics for a few years, and then they both decided to retire from work, dispense with the nanny, and bring Connie up themselves. They had been married for thirteen years at the time.

"Connie recalled being blissfully happy and feeling wanted and loved. She hid her damage for fear of rejection, and no one ever was supposed to find out about her past. Naturally the Blakes were party to some detail surrounding Connie's former ill treatment, but the local authorities who placed her in adoptive care made sure the minimum was disclosed probably as a matter of course and surely to protect Connie's dignity.

"The Blakes were great parents to start with and they were clearly very influential socialites. They threw huge parties and moved in all of the right circles. Yes, they were very strict most of the time, but they knew how to parent and actively supported Connie in her studies. They were immensely proud of her abilities. It was as if their dream child had been sent from above.

"Connie took some time, possibly years, to get used to it all.

"She not only had a real family now, but she lived in privileged surroundings and went on lavish foreign holidays. She was quiet and studious, tried not to make waves or get in the way. Most of Hillary Blake's friends had never met Connie as she shut herself away so as never to be a burden or a nuisance whenever the Blakes entertained. Now she looks back on it, she was protecting her position.

"If she did well at school and stayed out of trouble, she would be allowed to stay with this family. If she accidentally broke a glass in the kitchen, in her own mind she may have to leave. To go back to where she came from was her biggest fear. She didn't walk on egg shells, but she protected what she had and the only things she had of any value were a stuffed toy dog she called Dally and her new family.

"In the summer of 1998 when Connie was just sixteen, she sat for her advanced level exams at the private all-girls school she had attended with glee the past few years. To all except Connie's amazement and a full two years ahead of her class, she earned the top grade possible in all Five subjects and a place at Oxford University. Again, how proud Mr. and Mrs. Blake must have been? Connie would become one of the youngest girls in the country to gain a place at the most prestigious of all England's great universities.

"That summer should have been bliss for Connie, and it started out just great. But things didn't go that way for long.

"Just as Connie had started to contemplate a life worth living, Mrs. Blake was killed in a tragic accident while they were cycling in the South of France. Mr. Blake and Connie returned to England with the body, and everything changed overnight. Blake wasted no time at all and quickly descended into debauchery, drinking, drugs, and women of all shapes and sizes—but mostly prostitutes, very young prostitutes. Within a year of Hillary Blake's death, everything for Connie had changed.

"Connie guessed that the Blakes knew most of her past,' Connie said. 'I just think they didn't say anything in the hope that it was all forgotten. In reality, I could never forget it, but I was not going to speak of what had happened, and they were never going to ask.'

"Soon it was clear to Connie that Alan Blake knew much more than she had imagined he would and he began to show it in unwanted ways.

"Blake blamed Connie for the accident and told her as much immediately after the funeral. She had been the keen cyclist, after all. It had all been her idea—the new bikes they had bought together, the holiday and the day-trip that ended so tragically on that busy road. He decided to close himself away from the outside world, and Connie was back to servitude. The staff members they had were either sacked in a drunken rage or left of their own accord after his constant and unwanted sexual advances. So once again,

Connie was to cook, clean, wash, scrub, hoover, and before very long save enough energy to pleasure Blake. If she didn't, she would face the consequences.

"'He would say that he knew what a slut I had been and how many men I had had. He told me not to be so shy. If I ever refused him anything, I was punished. At first, the punishment was to spend a night locked in the kitchen sleeping on the stone floor. It was all like something out of *Oliver Twist*, but it was real. It was happening to me again. I remember how cold it was when I slept in the kitchen. When I wouldn't stop crying, he would get my old floppy-eared stuffed Dalmatian dog that I had had forever. He would just throw Dally at me and shout at me to shut up. I held that silly little stuffed dog for dear life night after night. I think it was the only thing that got me through it. I was seventeen years old, but there I was curled up with my little stuffed doggy as if I was eight.

"'What the hell had I done to deserve that again? I already knew I was worthless and dirty and used. I began to believe the past was my fault—or that what had happened to Mrs. Blake was my fault. Soon, just pleasuring him wasn't enough. I arrived home one night quite late. It was a bright moon-filled summer night. I had been out by the riverbank with friends. Boys and girls my age.

"'I walked up the garden path without a care in the world, but as I neared the house, I remembered what was probably waiting for me, and my smile faded away fast. Sure enough, he had been watching me from the house. I could hear the pornography on the TV as soon as I got in the door. He wasted no time at all. He came at me so fast that I had no time to react. Before I knew it, he was on me. I screamed and I struggled, but it was no use. He raped me right there on the hallway floor.

"Once he had broken that taboo Connie said Blake never looked back. It was as if he had been dying to do it for years, and now that he had, he was empowered. It never stopped after that. I almost decided to just take it forever. But one day, I somehow found the strength to say no. One night after he collected me from Oxford and drove me to a stranger's house. I can't even begin to tell you what that horrible, fat, strange man did to me while Blake watched and laughed.

"Blake said that the next time I said no to him, there would be three of them. He said he had a list of men he'd told about me. I understood all right. Only too well. That was going to be it for me forever, and it would get worse. So to his surprise, I decided there and then that he would never touch me again.'

"Connie made the strange and sadistic choice to be abused by many men rather than to be abused by Blake ever again—perhaps so she was at least able to make a choice and to be in charge for once. So she could be in control and defiant. So she could decide who would abuse her—or at least who would not—and be able to say no for once in her life.

"'Do you know what?' Connie said with tears streaming down her face. 'I won. It worked. I broke him.'

"The level of abuse ratcheted up over the next year or so. Blake knew that he couldn't physically attack Connie because she was fully grown and the ensuing fight would have left marks on both of them. So he tried as hard as he could to bring her back in line. He introduced her to stranger after stranger, and still she just took it.

"She said, 'I turned to him and said, Look at me. Look at this. You will never get this again—never.' She had beaten him. She had broken him. She had won.

"Mercifully for Connie, Alan Blakes' hold over her emotionally, physically and of course financially couldn't last forever. After replying to an advert in the local paper for a job with accommodation, Connie snuck out in the night and was finally away. She took nothing but the clothes she was standing in and fled. When I met her for the first time on that fateful day in 2002, she was a completely shattered and withdrawn twenty-one year old who lived above a Chinese restaurant in a small village not far from my house. She had been there two years washing dishes and cleaning floors most evenings and each weekend while she attended Oxford by day. She earned her food and a safe bed for the night but most of all her dignity.

"Blake never tried to contact Connie, probably in the hope that she would let sleeping dogs lie. Perhaps he was regretful—remorseful, even. Perhaps not. Connie decided not to do anything about Blake—for the time being, at least.

"When I asked her why she had never had Blake arrested, I felt so sorry for her when she replied that she had had so much bad stuff happen to her early on in life, and it had somehow continued to define her, so the last thing she wanted was to add to it.

"She said with tears in her eyes, 'By staying quiet and in the shadows I felt in control of what had happened to me. It was my secret and I would keep it until I decided not to. Back then I wanted peace. I wanted to be still, nondescript, and invisible. I chose to be silent.'

"After all Connie had told me about that sick bastard I thought to myself that Blake must have imagined he'd gotten away with it. A thought which almost burned my heart right out of my chest."

CHAPTER 18

Boating.

——

June 2005.
Peter.

James decided what he was going to do about Alan Blake and the picture of his old boat on the thirty-seven-minute train ride from London's Paddington Station to Maidenhead. It made the taxi ride from there to his house a pleasant place to catch some rest.

You see, although the news had come as a massive shock and although it was an almost unbelievable coincidence that Alan Blake might have known Steven South, it changed very little. James still didn't have Emma, and he never would find out what had happened to her because South was gone. What would have been the point of telling Laura? Or the police for that matter? What were they going to do? March around there and arrest Blake? For what? And at the back of his mind

James must have considered how any action against Blake would impact on Connie.

No. James decided to deal with the news himself when the time was right, so he hid the picture in an old shoe box in a "man drawer" at the back of the garage where it stayed for the best part of eight months.

As James and Laura lived so close to the beautiful River Thames, it was not uncommon, albeit they hadn't done it for some time, for them to rent a boat on any given Sunday, especially in the summer or when one of the regattas was on. So James aroused little suspicion when he announced what was planned for that sunny June day in 2005.

"I've rented a boat for the day, babe," James said to Laura.

"Lovely," she replied. "Where will we go?"

"I thought we would take it up to Henley early in the morning and go to the farmers' market. What do you think?" Laura thought it was a great way to spend the day, and so it was.

On one of those long nights in the pub, James said to me, "All the time I was hatching my plan, I never once felt I was being deceitful to Laura. I mean, I didn't want her to know about South and the boat just yet, and I didn't feel bad about keeping it from her, either. I know that probably doesn't make much sense. It's not that I was protecting her, although there was a bit of that. I just wasn't sure what I would find and what I would do if I found anything. I just wanted to take a look at first.

"So we slipped out of our mooring at Higginson Park in Marlow on a twenty-nine-foot renter that could just about do the speed limit of four knots. We left for the two-hour jaunt to Henley early enough to arrive at about eleven. It's a really pleasant trip, to be honest. I couldn't believe it had been at least a year since we had last done it. Lots of beautiful countryside to see and interesting, if tricky, locks to negotiate. We made our way upstream, passing the majestic weirs at Temple and Hambleden on the way. Laura and I got off the boat at Henley in good time but guess what Peter? The bloody farmers' market was on Saturdays, not Sundays."

"Anyway. To avoid completely wasting our time, Laura suggested we went to the local Waitrose super-market and bought some bread and cheese to eat on the way back. We had a quick couple of gin and tonics at The Angel, which, if you get the chance, Peter, is a great little pub right on the river at Henley Bridge. Then we headed back and I soon got to the real reason I was so inclined to rent a boat that day! On the return leg, the river takes small detours near the locks and weirs. We all use the same locks, of course, but the approaching traffic is diverted slightly to one side or the other. One such detour takes the downstream craft on a wide arc 'round an island and back to the main channel.

"I had long since handed over the controls to Laura and had set about preparing some drinks to accompany our cheese. To be honest, she is a better skipper than I am, and I am better at doing locks and boat drinks. As we rounded the island, I reached into my pocket and carefully removed the picture. I made sure that I was out of Laura's sight, and with my hands shaking, I looked at it.

"In the picture, the dark wood of Alan Blake's boat shone in the sunlight, and its distinctly new red ensign was frozen by the camera shutter for all time. The name, as if I needed to be reminded, was clear on the stern. The words 'Bisham Boot' were visible even on the faded old photo. The police evidence number and the date, 25 July 1987, were still discernable along the photo's bottom edge. The photo, which had possibly been donated by Blake himself in an attempt to appear helpful, had been taken from the other side of the narrow river, and the house was in the background. When I held it up to the landscape sliding by, it all lined up perfectly. In the photo was a moment frozen in time, and that moment was virtually unchanged from that day to this except that the boat was not there. There was the house where Alan Blake had lived and where he had done such terrible things to Connie. But no 'Bisham Boot'.

"I held the picture close to my side as I passed Laura with a kiss and set myself up on the long comfy bench behind her as we slowly steamed by the manicured hedges and the lawn of the magnificent redbrick house. The gardens were large enough to hold a football tournament, the house itself was set back and up. It reminded me of the sort of thing you'd see in old movies. The ones where ladies wear bonnets and don't carry their own parasols.

"Although the grass was newly mown, the house looked completely closed up. Large white shutters hid the old windows and doors from inquiring eyes. Climbing plants and ivy clung like spider webs to the sunniest walls. We approached the end of the property's imposing waterfront and were greeted by a riverside cutting. Two more well-kept hedges flanked the water that led up to Blakes' private boathouse. It was a real boathouse rather than a mere shed or roof over a private access to the river. You could have lived in it.

"As we passed at a steady three knots, I had about five seconds to glance unnoticed at the boathouse doors, which to my complete heart-stopping surprise began to open. I hastily replanted the photo in my pocket and began to panic. What was in there? What was coming out? Who was coming out? Could I get Laura to turn our boat around without a good excuse? In a flash of stupidity and the glow of three gins, I quickly managed to hatch some sort of a plan and there was little time to think of a better one. What had emerged from the boathouse doors was a large old dark-wood vessel. It had rounded the corner from the private slip and was turning its bow to begin following us. My heart was racing faster than is safe for a man of my age.

"Laura asked if I was all right. I said I was feeling a little seasick. That wasn't that much of a lie. I disappeared into the galley for a few seconds to get a drink of water and to quickly pen some words. We were approaching the last lock before Marlow, and so as usual, I volunteered to do the fending and the ropes. They were small, tight river locks that had been designed hundreds of years ago and had never really improved. Boats of all shapes and sizes were crammed in about four or five at a time, and then they were transferred up and down the steps in the river.

"There's a strict etiquette to get used to. The locks 'round here are manned, especially in the summer months, and the lockkeepers are a no-nonsense bunch. They usually don't care much for the renters, either. After all, we are the inexperienced lot most likely to ding a local's pride and joy.

"The entrance to the lock is like a filter lane. You approach it slowly and stay in a line. Once the gate is opened, you are guided in one by one, and you try not to collide with the other boats or with the lock gates themselves. Everybody does as they are told, and it usually passes without too much incident. So in we went. We were second on the left. The lockkeeper shouted and pointed. I quickly adjusted the grasp I had on the rope now securely around an old cast-iron bollard on the riverbank and the collision was narrowly averted.

"As the boat which had followed us was larger, she was ushered forward and away to our right side. Then the water began to be drained from the lock, and as it subsided, the boats started to slide on the stream of outrushing water. Someone shouted to take care. I handed the ropes to Laura and made for the bow in order to fend off the unmistakable stern of Bisham Boot.

"The owner had his back to me and was holding his own ropes. He was preoccupied with the small blue renter in front of him and the awful way in which it had tied off. Eagerly eying the stern of the blue boat in front of him, 'Bisham Boot' awaited the inevitable collision and the wrath of the lockkeeper. A quiet few seconds past by before, with a sudden rush of water, we each lurched again toward one another, I saw my opportunity and then it was done.

"The gates opened, and we proceeded out in an orderly fashion, which is what you are supposed to do. But with so many boats in such close proximity, it doesn't always go according to plan. His back was to me the whole time. The bow of the 'Bisham Boot' was tauntingly close to me, yet thankfully, it was travelling away about one knot faster than we were. There was a skipper about my age and build up front, and now on his seat, as yet unseen, lay an old police photograph. Hastily inscribed on its back were my contact details and the freshly inked words, 'I know about you and Steven South.'"

CHAPTER 19

INVITE.

———

Peter. 2008.

IT WAS JUNE OF 2008 and swelteringly hot in New York. Sandi and I had not seen the Foresters in a while after spending two Christmases in a row with the in-laws in America instead. Sandi's mum said that we were well overdue, and I guess she was right. I had kept in touch with James by e-mail, and by that time I knew about the return of the dreaded cancer. He was playing it down in his usual way, but it was back with a vengeance, this time as an aggressive secondary in his lungs.

Having chemotherapy for a second time must have been scary. The first time had been only a small dose. They had only given it to him "to be on the safe side." It's unusual for testicular cancer to spread and resurface a good few years later. It was bad luck, to say the least. This, then, was a bigger deal, and I could tell from the drop off in e-mails that James was not doing well. When we received a large official-looking envelope from the Foresters out of the blue, we feared it was bad news. So to open it and to immediately realize what it contained was both a relief and a wonderful surprise.

The card said, "Mr. and Mrs. Forester request the pleasure of your company at the wedding of Jake and Connie."

"August tenth, babe," I said to Sandi. "That's only about six weeks away. Can we go?"

Of course, there was never any doubt that we would go. We quickly had our bags packed. Sandi was on the Internet looking at Karen Millen dresses before I finished reading the invitation.

"All Saints' Church in Marlow for the service, and after that a posh-sounding reception at 'The Compleat Angler,' whatever that is."

That hot New York summer passed mercifully quickly, and before we knew it, we were back at JFK once again.

We arrived in the United Kingdom just as the sun came out. The wisecracks about how we had brought the weather with us started immediately. Apparently, it had been raining constantly for the past nine months. I thought that was pretty standard, to be honest. If the sun is shining, August in leafy old England can be as blissful as anywhere in the world. Probably the most blissful. And so it was.

The only fly in the ointment was the accommodation. There wasn't any. You see, it turns out that leafy old England is a very popular place in August when the sun is shining. Plus, Marlow is a small town, and a well-known family was hosting a wedding right smack in its center. We dearly wanted to stay at 'The Compleat Angler' where the reception was taking place. On the Internet, it looked like a fantastic riverside hotel, but unfortunately, everyone else wanted to stay there too. The invites must have taken an extra day or two to get to us, because even though we rang the hotel that very day, it was already full. After looking and asking around, we realized that we were never going to get a room in Marlow in August, wedding or no wedding.

Naturally, James asked us to stay at his house, which was so kind. We almost said yes, thinking that it might have been our last resort. You see, it didn't seem right to be there taking up a room in their home and getting in the way. Especially because we were not family.

Then Sandi hit on the genius idea of renting a houseboat. It was more like a large river cruiser that you could sleep on, according to the brochure, but it was a great solution to our accommodation problem. And to cap it all off, it turned out that 'The Compleat Angler' was directly opposite the church on the other riverbank and it even had overnight births for boats. What could have possibly gone wrong?

So we had a warm bed, albeit a floating one, and it was right outside the church and the reception venue, all of which were within a short walk of the Foresters' house.

We collected the boat from Hobbs of Henley on the Monday before the wedding, and after much too short an induction, we were handed the keys to a brand-new ten-meter gin palace. OK, it was in the old riverboat style, like the American "Grand Banks" boats, but it was new with modern conveniences nonetheless.

After not too long at all, I got the hang of driving the thing, if "driving" is the correct nautical term. We stocked her up with food and wine from the local shops and headed with some trepidation toward the first lock. Now, I don't know if you have ever heard an American woman swear at the top of her lungs before, but suffice it to say that it was a good thing that the kids had stayed in the United States. Silence followed at the next two locks, and then Sandi decided to talk to me again.

"You could have fucking killed us back there," was all she said. And then the silent treatment resumed. I thought I had the thing relatively under control. But I was very wrong. Then I had the wrath of the lock-keepers to deal with all the way down the river. Each lockkeeper had clearly phoned ahead to the next one to warn them of the impending doom. We were worried about killing ourselves not to mention the cost of repairs to the once-new boat we had rented.

I didn't think it looked that bad, but when I delivered it back the following Monday, the bloke had a fit. Seven thousand dollars to go to a wedding! "Never mind, it's only money," is what Sandi says I should have said. What I actually said almost got me arrested.

The drama over, we moored up for the night about halfway to Marlow as it was getting near nine o'clock, and then we shoved off, as they say, to Marlow in the morning.

We were expected for lunch at the Foresters' house, and luckily, we made good speed. That time, the locks were quieter, and the wind was lighter. Add to that some assistance from Sandi, the able sailor, and it went off without a hitch. We followed the directions Jim had supplied and moored up alongside a quiet riverbank on the east edge of the village. We made our way along a narrow grass footpath, across a small open field, and through a newly painted garden gate, which had some party balloons tied to it so we wouldn't get lost. It wasn't until I swung open the clearly new gate that what I had just done dawned on me.

James had the gateway in the hedge installed especially for us. He had done it so we didn't have to moor up a mile away, or walk the long route around to the front door. That meant that I was the first man in nearly two decades to arrive by boat and to walk the path to the Foresters' back garden. No one else had done it since South had. James met me halfway across the garden, and no words were needed. He knew I knew. It showed in our faces. We just hugged and cried a little. Then before it all got too out of hand, we were upbeat again. He hugged Sandi, and we were in the house in a flash. We all lovingly exchanged greetings and quaffed our glasses of champagne.

As always, Laura looked fabulous, and just like the last time, Sandi was whisked away upstairs within minutes so the two of them could cackle about dresses and makeup and whatever it is they did under the din of the hair dryer. I have always had the good sense not to inquire.

Jake arrived soon after with his stunning bride-to-be, of course. They had rented a flat about six months after that fateful New Year's Eve and had been living together for about a year just a couple of miles outside the center of town. I was near the living room window as they walked across the road hand in hand.

Someone said, "That's a handsome couple." I was a small boy when I first heard the saying and understood it to mean that the subjects in question were both nice to look at and were clearly devoted to each other. It meant "good-looking people who were sickeningly in love." It's an old-fashioned saying, but there had never been a more worthy recipient of the compliment than those two.

All Saints' Church was packed. I had never seen anything remotely like it. Apart from in *Four Weddings and a Funeral*, of course. The English do know how to do a proper wedding. Everyone was in top hats and tails. The ladies were in their finest frocks and best broad-brimmed hats. The sun was shining on all of us that day.

The groom was as calm as a cucumber. His best man, Glen, was standing next to him. The traditional tune began to play as we all stood and politely craned our necks to see Connie triumphantly arrive through the huge oak doors at the end of the church. She was the most wonderful sight as the afternoon sunlight framed the silhouette of her long white dress.

I had to raise my hand to shield my eyes from the glare and squint to see the frame of a man holding her arm. As they drew closer, the doors behind them closed, and we could all see the proud and beaming gentleman who had the honor of giving Connie away. James wiped away the tears as soon as he lovingly handed Connie to Jake and moved slowly away to his left. He was the proudest father I had ever seen. After taking his seat next to Laura, he turned to give me a wink.

I did wonder what some might think, James giving Connie away to his son as if he were her father, but to us few it was perfectly natural. I also had a good look around to see if Alan Blake was there, but I didn't even know what he looked like.

It was a quintessential English wedding in a classic country church filled with the smell of summer flowers. What a day! The reception was across the river from the church. The river flowed slowly in the summer and couldn't have been more than eighty meters wide. The bridge between the banks stood majestically beside the church. We would soon take a short but spectacular walk from one side to the other. Or at least I thought we would.

After we disentangled ourselves from the mass of flowers and pews and wiped away the tears of joy, we waited to congratulate the couple. Then there were photos to take in the time-honored tradition. I am sure that it all took way too long for the little ones. But soon enough, we were walking over the old iron bridge to 'The Compleat Angler'.

The place made quite the statement—it was posh and imposing, and it was the very best location for a wedding party. Hell, even a cup of tea on the covered terrace in the winter would have been a treat. Laid before us out on the sunny riverside lawn and for the entire town to see were tables with the finest white linens and chairs with slipcovers that reached the ground with huge dark-red bows on their backs. There were matching dark-red rose petals everywhere. Even the band members, who were friends of Jake's and who, judging by their neck tattoos, were accustomed to less salubrious venues, wore smart black suits and dark-red trilby hats.

Naturally, we all assumed the bride and groom had gone before us in the waiting limousine. After all, we had waved and cheered as they had gotten in and had watched as it drove them around the back of the church and toward the road that would bring them over the bridge. But no. Once each and every guest was assembled by the river's edge and had a glass suitably filled with pink champagne, the fanfare began to sound. Something spectacular was afoot.

The bride and groom emerged once more from the church, waving and smiling from across the water. Downstream, a majestic old paddle steamer approached them. It was decked out in red ribbon and flowers, and there was white smoke billowed above. She pulled up alongside the church, and the happy couple embarked with little fuss but with another huge cheer from us all.

James was perfectly placed above them in the center of Marlow's old iron bridge and was capturing it all on the camcorder he had purchased especially for the occasion. Beside him, quite a number of tourists and slow-to-move guests watched in awe as the steamer inched across the river toward us. Then, just as the craft neared the middle of the river, a man pushed in beside James, he leaned over the rail, and let something drop from his outstretched hand.

It was Alan Blake. He was looking right at James, and not at the happy couple, and what he dropped from the bridge on that perfect summer's day was a photograph of an old wooden boat. No one except James seemed to notice.

James couldn't have failed to notice because as the video camera captured the steamboat below him, the fluttering picture spun down toward the dark water, turning as it did like a leaf on the breeze. It was right in the center of the frame. James looked up from the viewfinder to see the back of a man wheeling away through the crowd. There was no time for a confrontation, and it appeared that neither man wanted one on that day.

Bemused and a little shaken, James continued on his path along the iron bridge and down the steps to the lawn. He arrived just in time to capture the moment we had all been eagerly awaiting—the moment when the new Mr. and Mrs. Forester alighted from the steamer and joined the adoring crowd of friends and relatives. The remainder of the day passed without incident or distraction. The food and wine were to die for, and there was good company and great weather to boot. Sandi even managed to get me on the dance floor toward the end of the night.

As is customary, I think on these sort of occasions, James and I were the last to leave and if it's not customary, then maybe we started something in style.

An hour earlier, I had escorted Sandi to our luxurious floating accommodation, which was tied up beside the hotel's east gardens and directly adjacent to the river weir. The sound of the constantly cascading waters would have sent anyone off to a peaceful sleep.

James and I had one or two last drinks, and as we sat together on a large brown-leather Chesterfield sofa, the silence after the day's excitement swept over us and across the room to the open window. We both sighed that sigh at the same time. The sigh of satisfaction. The sigh that says, "Phew, that was a cracking day, but I'm sort of glad it's all over."

"Alan Blake was on the bridge next to me," James said.

"No way!" I said in shock,

"Did he say anything to you?"

"It's not what he did or didn't say Pete. Can you take me for a ride in your boat tomorrow? Just you and me. I've got some stuff to tell you, and there's something I want to do."

CHAPTER 20

BISHAM.

———

Peter. August 2008.

W<small>E WERE MOORED UP ON</small> the river below the Marlow lock. Our path to the center of town demanded that we set off downstream at about eleven in the morning. The riverbank to our north was actually an island, and once we figured that out, our confusion abated. We soon found ourselves around the other side and back in the main part of the Thames.

"It's right there, babe," shouted our first mate, Sandi. And, of course, so it was.

We were never more than a few hundred yards from the banks of the river at Pergola Field, where Sandi and I had pulled up many times the last week to walk to James and Laura's back garden. This meant that we were very early for lunch, but no one seemed to mind. Most of our companions were still in clothes they had slept in by the look of it. Connie and Jake had walked over the town bridge from the hotel and arrived at the house at about the same time we did.

Sandi said, "We should have given you a lift. We could have done with a navigator."

In any case we were all in fine form apart from our heads.

Lunch was pleasant, and smiles crept on our faces from time to time as we remembered small details from the day before.

James made some excuse to Laura and the others about boys needing some 'man time' together as we hadn't seen each other in years and I was soon to be heading back to New York. No one seemed to care anyway, so we slipped out of the house alone at about three that afternoon and set off for my renter.

The weather was not as good as it had been for the wedding, but rarely have I seen such great weather in England as we had the day before. It was still warm, but it was cloudier, and there was a fresh breeze from the southwest. I remember thinking that a little chop would spray us, no doubt.

"Where to, Jim?" I asked without reply.

James assumed control as I loosened the mooring lines and pushed us out. James began to take us upstream toward the lock and on through the town. We passed under the iron road bridge by the hotel and out past the park. He steered, and we progressed at a slow-but-steady four knots, which was actually far less thanks to the river flowing against us, but we didn't seem to be in a hurry to get anywhere.

James began to bring me up to date. He told me the whole story about the Bisham Boot, about the picture, and the link between South and Blake. I began to get a little concerned. James was positive there was a link between the two men, but I was not so sure. The police were confident that there was not any link, and it had been over three years since James deposited the picture in the back of Blake's boat.

James's mood changed for the worse each time we mentioned Blake's name. Of course, I knew about the way he had treated Connie, most of it anyway, and I hated him for it almost as much as James did. But naturally, there was an added dimension to it for James—Emma.

Before too long, we had open fields on our right and huge mansions and country hotels on our left. We passed the gigantic Bisham Abbey, which became an elite sports training center. I think that even the English football team has stayed there. In no time at all, we shot up the next lock at Hurley and pushed on through a few more river bends and past some blissful countryside. Then we turned for home, and I wondered if James had changed his mind. We hadn't gone far back toward Marlow and I confess I lost my bearings a little as we skirted around a small island or two then we pulled up to the riverbank on our left and secured a line at the stern against the flow of the river, which seemed desperate to take us home.

Jim returned from the galley with two cold beers, settled himself on the open side of the boat next to me, gazed out across about forty meters of water to the opposite bank.

Then he calmly took a sip of his beer and gestured to the opposite bank. "There," he said. Pointing with his bottle.

I looked and asked what was "there."

"That, my Yankee friend, is where he took Emma. That's the house," James added.

"Hang on," I said. "That's the house? The house that looks like a hotel? The biggest one of all—the one right opposite us?"

James cut in, "Yup, that's where South took Emma. That's where he was supposedly painting the boat-house. That boathouse there," Jim added as he pointed at the old redbrick building with huge white painted doors which opened onto the water. It was set back up a private cut of the river and was bigger than most of the houses around there. The main house was also set back from the river about fifty meters. It filled the skyline. I thought it was probably the biggest and the most expensive property in that or any other part of the world. My jaw dropped a little, but James continued.

"That is the house. That is the house where Blake and his wife lived. That is the house where Connie lived, where she was brutalized by that bastard. That's the house where Blake still lives, and the boat is still in there."

He pointed first to the mansion, and then with even more disgust, he pointed to the boathouse. James was getting agitated, and I began to get really worried. I thought he was going to throw the bottle across the river, and I think that if we had been closer, he would have.

"You really think Blake knew South, don't you?" I asked, hoping beyond hope that Jim would reconsider.

But his reply confirmed it. "I know he did. It's too much of a coincidence. Paedophiles know each other, especially now with the Internet. A guy doesn't just live in your boathouse while painting it and use your boat if you don't even know him. They had friends in high places—the police even said so. No one thought the couple could be involved with a child snatcher—I mean, look at the place. So 'make no waves' was the decision. I mean, if the police had accused him and had ruined his reputation for nothing, they would have gotten it in the neck. People would have lost their jobs and promotions. It's an 'old boys' club' for sure. The fucking commander personally came here to see Blake, and then he brushed it under the police station carpet."

"OK," I said. "Even if you are right, what are we doing here, James?"

And just like that, he calmed down and slumped on the bench seat next to me. I knew then that we were not there for any reason, except perhaps so James could vent a little. That was a relief. Probably for the both of us.

By the time we got back to the house, it was early evening. Everyone was in such high spirits that no one even asked where we had been. We had some food and a few more drinks before sadly Sandi and I had to say our good-byes and head back to the boat. We wanted to give them some peace and let them have a rest from all the visitors and eating and drinking, so we slipped away at about nine o'clock. We still had to sail back up to Henley early in the morning to return the boat and collect our car, and then we had to get ourselves to Heathrow in time for our flight home. Luckily it was still light at that time of year as we staggered along that narrow grassy path from the back garden of Jim's house to the waiting boat.

When I think back to that blissful wedding and the afternoon spent on the water, I know I would have savored it more and given him a much bigger hug as we parted if only I had known that it was going to be the last time I would ever see James alive.

CHAPTER 21

WILL TO LIVE

——

Peter. October, November 2008.

I T WAS ONLY ABOUT SIX weeks after that blissful wedding of August 2008 when James phoned and excitedly told me about Alan Blake's sudden death.

"The fucking stupid bastard fell down his own stairs last week!" is roughly how Jim put it. For an Oxford professor he always did have a way with words.

James seemed to be genuinely aggrieved that Blake was dead. I'm pretty sure he wanted a nastier end for him. It was all too easy, and what Blake had done to Connie would now stay buried with him. And of course, any chance of finding out the real truth about Blake's connection to Steven South and maybe even to Emma had disappeared too.

The gardener had found his body at the foot of the stairs. The house had been filthy and partly closed up. He had been a virtual recluse for some time, and his twisted body may well have lay there with a broken neck for at least a week before it was discovered.

The tradesman wanted to be paid, you see, and wouldn't take no response to his knock at the door for an answer. He peered through the dirty ground-floor windows at the back of the house in an "I know you are in there" type of way. He got more than he had bargained for.

The house was a mess—it was dusty and dirty as Blake had long since dispensed with the cleaner. The rooms were mostly shut up, and he lived in the kitchen beside the huge AGA stove, which being constantly on, was then the only heating in the place. Since the dogs had gone, his only company was whiskey. Scotch was a friend he had made when Hillary was killed, and he had turned to it more and more as the years went by. The room where Connie had spent most of her formative years was preserved like a shrine, and it was the only tidy part of the house.

The bathrooms were dirty, and the toilets were dry and smelled like the sewers they were connected to. The windows hadn't been cleaned in years, and the fateful stairs from which Blake had cascaded to his demise were covered in stacks of papers. On each step was a stack that was the height of the next step. Two or three piles and a bottle of whiskey had been knocked over, and the culprit was therefore only too obvious. The coroner's certificate was issued within the week and he'd said something like, "Accidental death as a result of a fall, which was most likely due to alcohol intoxication and the piles of paper stacked dangerously on the stairs."

The funeral took place shortly thereafter. It was quite a lavish affair. He had been, after all, a very wealthy and well-known man and had once been a pillar of the community. The eulogy was lovingly read by his brother-in-law, his closest living relative, and it included Blake's long list of accolades, most of which had involved his work and wealth. Few had to do with his personal life. Alan Blake was lowered into the ground beside his wife on a dark, rainy October evening. The sun set ceremonially as he disappeared beneath the cold, wet ground. There were well-wishers but not that many. People from the neighborhood and from his former business went to pay their respects. One by one, most of them stepped forward to throw a handful of earth onto the lid of the coffin in the time-honored tradition. As the masses in black moved through the rain toward the car park, their dark umbrellas up and their faces down, a lone figure was watching from the trees near the edge of the churchyard. A tall, slender woman with jet-black hair, standing alone, in a deliberately disrespectful bright-red cloak.

———

The last will and testament of Mr. Alan Reginald Blake was read out a month later in November of 2008 at the office of the solicitors Bennet, Sidford, and Giles. Their premises were located in a drab 1970s concrete building near the center of Maidenhead. It was surrounded by multilevel car parks and similarly dilapidated structures all of which were evidently erected in haste after the destruction of the second world war bombing.

There were only two benefactors whose presence Mr. Sidford requested in writing. They were Mr. William Brown, who was Hillary Blake's brother, and a young newlywed by the name of Constancia Forester.

After exchanging pleasantries and offering them coffee, Mr. Sidford began the process of listing the total assets in an orderly and matter-of-fact way.

Blake had cars, property, shares, cash, investments, more property abroad, bonds, pensions, boats, and even a plane. The more Mr. Sidford went on, the more intently Mr. Brown listened, and the more uncomfortable Connie felt. Brown was actually rubbing his hands together the entire time whilst Connie was chewing on her top lip. It went on for seventeen minutes. The solicitor diligently listed some twenty-five properties (five of which were in foreign countries like Barbados and the Isle of Man), four boats, one small jet, nine cars, a racehorse, shares, investments, and cash. Lots of cash. Nothing had been valued, of course—that was done much later by the press. It became local folklore. After all, you can imagine that an entire estate worth over five hundred million pounds would attract attention.

The investments Blake had made, many of which were in central London property, had increased in worth tenfold. The huge house in Marlow, which he and Hillary had purchased for six million pounds in the early nineties, was now thought to be worth well over thirty.

Once the assets had been described in detail, Mr. Sidford sat forward, cleared his throat, turned to Mr. Brown and Mrs. Forester, and read the last will and testament, which had been prepared, signed, and witnessed in that very office just two years earlier.

"I, Alan Reginald Blake, do leave to Mr. William Brown, the beloved brother of my dearly departed wife, Hillary, my villa in Spain, my dogs, if I am survived by any, and my beloved riverboat, *Bisham Boot*. The rest of my estate, I leave to my one and only daughter, Connie, who I will never be able to repay."

Now, Mr. Brown had been hoping for a bit more, of course, but he was a simple man of very limited means, and it turned out he was into boats. He improved his lot in life significantly by selling the villa in Marbella, Spain, for eight million euros the following year.

Connie had not been expecting anything whatsoever, to say the least. She had imagined that he had invited her just to torment her. To make the solicitor read it all out and announce he had left her a goldfish—that sort of thing. It would take some getting used to. She remembered living a privileged life when she was a young girl, and before it had all gone so very, very badly, she had been used to the finer things in life. But that had been years ago. Lots had happened since then, and she had deliberately almost forgotten about her childhood. She wasn't really sure what to feel—whether to laugh or cry. So she cried, and then she laughed. A lot.

Mr. Sidford first congratulated Mr. Brown as he politely showed Hillary's brother the door, then he turned his devoted attention to Connie. Of course there would be no need to discuss our fees at this time, he probably said as he let slip that her share was worth, in their unqualified opinion, four or five hundred million pounds. Connie Blake was now one of the wealthiest women in England, and she had to take a seat and some water before attempting to leave.

Connie had arrived in Maidenhead that afternoon by bus because she didn't know how to drive. She was driven home by a chauffeur, whom the solicitors had hired in advance. They had known something life changing was about to happen to one of their newest and most valuable customers. Connie was about to call Jake on the way home, but she decided that it was the sort of thing which needed to be said face to face. She knew he would be home from work by the time she arrived back, and they were supposed to have their usual Chinese take-away night at James and Laura's house. And so that was where she went.

She knew that as soon as the huge black Mercedes limo pulled up, James, Laura, and Jake would know something was afoot, so Connie got out and walked the last hundred yards. It gave her valuable time to think and to breathe it all in. They were all in the kitchen. James had been in and out of hospital for more chemotherapy the past few days. This morning being his last, he was very glad to be home. Although his overall heath was deteriorating, he was still in good spirits. Laura was organizing some warm plates for the food. Jake was only just in from another mundane shift at the local sports center where he had been employed as a swimming coach on minimum wage for the past two years.

Connie walked in slowly and set down the flimsy shopping bag she had been carrying around all day containing nothing but a bottle of mineral water she had not touched. They all turned to her and stood for what seemed like ages before James said, "Well." To which Connie responded with a disbelieving shake of her head, "He left it all to me! The bastard left it all to me! Five hundred million pounds Sidford says! He left it to me."

Instead of shouting for joy or laughing or congratulating her, they were all just silent. Everyone was just looking at each other and back at Connie. Then they hugged her.

Laura brought them all back to earth by exclaiming that the food was getting cold, and with that, they began to laugh. They spent a comparatively normal evening together under the circumstances, eating their Chinese takeout and drinking warm beer. Jake waited an entire hour before asking Connie if it was OK for him to jack in his crappy job, which drew more laughter and a huge hug from Connie. James was the only one who couldn't quite snap out of it. He just kept looking at Connie and Jake, shaking his head and saying "perfect" over and over again.

———

For a long time, Connie didn't really know how to feel about it all. Was it dirty money? Was she a giant hypocrite? James appeared to be conflicted about it all too, but deep down, he was glad that the bastard was gone and that Connie and Jake would have the benefit of his money. Everyone could have a drink on Blake and spit the finest champagne on the bastard's grave, is how James put it to me when he called to fill me in on it all.

In time, Connie too got used to the idea. In fact, it didn't take long. James was rapidly getting very sick. He pleaded with her and Jake to take it all and to enjoy their lives, if only as a gift to him. It was his dying wish to see the two of them happy, and what could have been better than spending Blake's hard-earned money along the way? And so they did.

CHAPTER 22

HOME FROM HOME.

———

Peter. 2009.

THE DECISION TO MOVE INTO the big Marlow riverside house which Blake had so dramatically vacated was not an easy one. Connie had lived there for many years as a teenager, not many of which held fond memories. Jake worried that in its current state it could turn out to be an unwanted money pit. In the end it was Laura who unexpectedly convinced them to go for it when she pointed out how vulnerable they were to unwanted press intrusion in their current one-bedroom apartment. Connie knew what Laura really meant was all the female attention Jake had been getting. Jake had become somewhat of a minor celebrity in the town due to his good looks and newfound wealth. Not that he flashed the cash or in any way encouraged admirers, but that Christmas was interesting to say the least.

Most people just wanted to know if the rumors were true and not having many friends meant Jake didn't have to go to too many Christmas parties where he would inevitably have to explain himself. Some so-called friends started showing up at the apartment in need of help in some way or another. Most were young girls!

Connie announced they were moving in immediately, and that was the end of that argument.

Spring was on its way and so was something else.

On January third of 2009 Connie had her twelve-week scan in complete secret and then called another of the now famous Chinese takeout evenings at James and Laura's place.

James was in tears within seconds, and Jake hugged his mum so tight she nearly passed out. It was a baby boy due in June, and everyone was understandably over the moon.

Now they really needed a bigger apartment. And so they got the keys from Mr. Sidford the following weekend and Connie swung open the huge old doors once again.

The first thing she did was announce to Jake's relief that the name had to go. Alan and Hillary Blake had called the big house "money tree park," which had always sounded pretentious to Connie and probably everyone else in the town. From now on it would be known as "Forest Grange."

There was much to do to the tired and dusty old place and no time like the present, so they began their work the following week. Connie and Jake used a local world-renowned firm that had recently been a victim of the economic downturn. They were highly skilled and extremely expensive, but they were, for the first time in years, available.

An esteemed architect from London by the name of Gill Greenfield was immediately hired as project designer and supervisor; he had the good sense to be gentle when guiding his employers through what would become extensive renovations. Jake was keen to keep as much of the original character of the place as possible, but as you can imagine, Connie was very keen to see a more contemporary finish. She wanted some of the memories gone for good. They had a brief but heated argument. She won. The first time Connie walked through the door must have been a very interesting experience for her. So much had gone on in that house.

She arrived with Jake, and they entered through the huge double-oak doors together. He thought about carrying her over the threshold, but he missed the opportunity and was glad that he had. The place was still a mess, even though a team of nine cleaners had been there for a week. They walked slowly around some of the huge ground floor and then out to the magnificent garden.

Thankfully, the gardener was still doing his job, but he hadn't been paid in two or three months. I guess he had just banked on the fact that someone would show up one day and assumed that he had better be busy doing his job if they did or he could forget about the back pay. The lawn wasn't lush at that time of year, but nevertheless the well-planned stripes led them down to the water's edge. From there, they turned to survey the enormity of it all.

The boathouse was locked up, but through the glass door they could see that the *Bisham Boot* was still there. Connie said she would call the solicitors in the morning and have it removed. She knew it upset James. Jake chatted to Bill the gardener who had emerged from a potting shed to meet his new employer. Bill waited until the lady of the house had gone before worrying the master with his remuneration predicament. He also mentioned maybe ten times that he was the one who had found poor Mr. Blake. Jake assured him of his finances and said that the lady of the house was actually the master of the house.

Connie had gone back inside the house and up the stairs; she passed the spot where Blake had slipped to his death without even a shudder. She went around the sweeping staircase and along to her old bedroom. It was, of course, the size of the entire first floor of an average house. It was still much as she had left it. The cleaners had done a fine job. It seemed so strange to be standing there all those years later. Everything was the same but so very different.

Then she remembered her favorite stuffed dog, the floppy old Dalmatian she had gotten at Disneyland when she was twelve. It had been with her ever since. It had been on her bed waiting for her every night without fail. Later, when things got really bad, it was her savior. It was the only thing she had missed after leaving in such a hurry. But Dally was the only thing not in its place. It had always been on her pillow. She hadn't been able to sleep without it. She and Jake searched the entire house, but that floppy-eared stuffed Dalmatian was the only thing missing.

Connie had all the money in the world, but what she wanted more than anything at that moment was her silly old Dally. She imagined that Blake had probably destroyed it in a temper as revenge for Connie leaving the way she did. Whatever he did with it and like so much of Blake's life, it couldn't be undone now.

For obvious reasons, they completely changed many of the rooms. They had walls taken down. Bathrooms put in. The old Blake matrimonial bedroom became a lavish guest suite. It was one of three, even though they couldn't name three people they would have as guests.

Before very long and as the impending addition to the family became more obvious, the plans for the room next to their own bedroom changed from a his-and-hers walk-in dressing room to a baby's nursery. The three huge rooms beyond that became a lavish apartment intended for when James and Laura stayed over.

To the west of the main house was a tennis court which was not in too bad a state. The pavilion overlooking it was in a far worse condition and had long since been reemployed as a much less dignified store for broken old lawn mowers.

To the east near the boathouse were two large cottages which flanked the long driveway. These had been staff lodges in the distant past, and Jake would eventually have them lovingly restored and modernized and the first occupants were the long-suffering gardener and his elderly mother.

Unfortunately for Sandi and me, much like the past couple of years, Christmas 2008 came and went in New York. We had been over that summer for the wedding after all, not to mention that Jazmine and Fay were by then about sixteen and eighteen years old. You try getting girls that age away from their boyfriends and see how far you get. In reality Sandi's father's health wasn't great and we couldn't afford the flights.

So we relied heavily on our regular e-mails from James, Laura, and thankfully Jake, who we had become close friends with.

By March of 2009 the e-mails from James became less regular, and his health deteriorated. The secondary cancer had spread further and faster than they had predicted it would, and sadly I soon learned that there would be no more treatments. It was the end for James Forester, and he knew it. He had made arrangements. He was ready.

The baby boy, who was to be named Jimmy after his granddad, was due in June. No one really expected James to make it to see his first grandchild, but they underestimated his will. James didn't just make it to the birth. He also made it to the delivery ward. He staggered along the corridors of the hospital that he himself resided in. He arrived unannounced. It was a great and pleasant surprise, although his doctor, who caught up with him a few minutes later, told him off. James was still in his bedgown having decided to follow Laura after she had just visited him, even though Laura had said she would bring the baby along to see James later that afternoon.

He was the first to hold little Jimmy Finn Forester—everyone insisted that he should be. Seated comfortably next to Connie, James hid his pain well. The midwife returned from the next room after taking Jimmy's weight and measurements and giving him a little rubdown. As far as everyone in that room was concerned, he was the most treasured cherub who had ever graced the earth.

He was a beauty. He was nine pounds, and he had long legs and black hair. Connie had the little man all wrapped up in a new woolen blanket which had been knitted especially for him by his great grandma.

James had used up all of his strength, a plethora of drugs, and resolve he hadn't known he had to make it to that moment, but now he was done.

He passed away that night in Laura's arms, just the way they both would have wanted it. Sandi and I were on the next plane to England. Jake sent a chauffeur to collect us from Heathrow airport, which was a very nice touch. Everyone was at the big house and I only wished we could have been there in better circumstances, because it was like something out of *Downton Abbey*. It had a long tree-lined drive and immaculate lawns, and the river meandered by. James would have loved it, I thought. To see the family together in such a setting.

It was naturally a sad time, but we put on brave faces and all of us, Connie and Sandi included, had typically British stiff upper lips because James would have insisted on it. We were immediately introduced to the new arrival, and Sandi hardly let him go for the next week. At times, and especially during the funeral when little Jimmy was evidently way more upset than everyone else, Connie was glad she had Sandi to cuddle Jimmy in the churchyard. We all stayed at Forest Grange, which by then had its new look and name. No expense had been spared on the renovations, which were still ongoing. The house and its new occupants looked amazing. James would have been so proud. There was Connie, still only twenty seven years old and she had it all. Surrounded by family and friends, ignoring the builders and the dust, it was at that moment almost a fairytale ending to the story. Little did we know!

CHAPTER 23

ALL SAINTS' AGAIN.

———

Peter. July 2009.

THE FUNERAL WAS HELD ON a warm Friday morning in July of 2009. That time, the mood was very
different in Marlow's All Saints' Church, even though
the sun did shine on the righteous once again. James
wanted it kept very simple, and so it was. There were
no gushing eulogies and only one hymn. There were
a few simple words and fewer and simpler flowers. It
was fine. Naturally, there was black and tears and sor-
row and reflection, but it wasn't somber. Just how he
wanted it to be.

He was laid to rest outside in the sunshine, and
following a touching internment ceremony, we were
once again able to walk across the beautiful old iron
bridge. We could stand together, look back across
the river with a glass raised aloft and say, "Good-bye,
Jim." And so we did just that, more than once.

I awoke on Saturday to another lovely sunny day. After breakfast and a brisk walk along the river to clear my head, I found my way into the center of Marlow and to the open doors of a busy lunchtime at our old watering hole, 'The Carpenters Arms'.

It had been a while, and I had never been there in the sunlight before, but it was the same old pub where I had first met James and where we had become close friends. The same old pub where James had begun his amazing story and where the next chapter was unexpectedly about to begin.

You see, a week or so before James passed away, I had received a very cryptic e-mail from him. It was out of the blue and out of character. It was so intriguing that I had to make a huge effort to conceal it from everyone.

It read;

Dear Peter,

I hope you are well. Not long to go now, I am afraid. Actually, I am not afraid, but you know what I mean. I hope very much that you will be able to get over here when the time comes. I have left arrangements for the funeral with Laura and Jake, so I don't want you to worry. No eulogy, please, mate. You're off the hook there.

When it's all done (and not before, please, promise me that!) I want you to go to our old pub (you know which pub) for one last beer. Only have one beer, because after that you'll need to head to Maidenhead station.

If you can't make it to the funeral, I will totally understand, but in that case, go next Christmas. Go when you can, mate, just like we used to do together. Only this time, tell whoever is behind the bar your name and ask for the key. They will know what you mean. It's in my old pewter tankard, which I hope will still be hanging there in twenty years' time. (PS, I told Dave that you can use my tankard anytime you'd like.)

All the best, old friend. I somehow doubt I will see you again. I trust you with this task, although I can't explain its importance here. You will see when you get there.

I think you will know exactly the right things to do and say when the time comes. I am sure I was right all along about you and Sandi, and you can paint me in whatever light you like, I can take it.

Thanks for all the laughs and for being such a great listener.

Good luck!

James.

Naturally, I replied to his e-mail and asked what the hell he was on about, but he never elaborated—in fact, he never replied at all. So there I was. There was the tankard, hanging on its usual brass hook. I had my beer served in it for old times' sake and sipped it while examining what appeared to be a locker key. I thought it rude not to, so I drank the beer as fast as an American could. To be honest, I wasn't sure if drinking the pint might have been significant, so I did as I was told. Then I paid and left for the nearest taxi with my heart racing in anticipation.

The taxi ride to the station took only thirty-five minutes, but it felt much longer. I wondered what the hell it was all about. I'd seen that sort of thing in old James Bond movies set in East Germany or the USSR but not in a pub in Marlow. But there was the numbered key that only I would know was for a locker at Maidenhead station. A battered, old red key. Why hadn't he just posted it to me? Then I was really excited. Anyway, I arrived, so I went in and spoke to the first person I saw in a high-visibility vest. And before I knew it, I was standing in front of a gigantic line of lockers.

One hundred twelve. Red. But they were all blue.

"Upstairs, mate," said the man next to me.

Thankfully, it was quite common for people to stand looking bemused with their key in their hand, only to find out they were on the wrong floor. So I went up the dirty old staircase as fast as I could. Red lockers—that was a good start, I thought. Sixty-six. Ninety-six. One hundred six. One hundred twelve. One hundred twelve, red. There it was.

Maidenhead station. One hundred twelve, red. Holy shit, I thought, this is good. I think I may have actually said it out loud. My heart was pounding so fast that it was probably dangerous. My hand was shaking, and I was sure I was being watched. For a moment, I paused and looked around before realizing that it was bound to look suspicious. Was I actually being watched—followed by the police or the mafia, for God's sake? What if the second I put the key in the lock, I was jumped by a SWAT team? Christ, this is stupid, I thought. I had to just open the dam thing. Then I had a plan. I decided to walk away again for a bit or put the key in a different lock. But my hand was up, and the key was on its way to its destination. I was so intrigued that I couldn't stop myself.

In slid the key, nice as pie. After a half turn, it was open. I tried again not to look around or act suspicious, but I had no idea what I was afraid of. Inside on the dusty bottom shelf, there was a small white envelope and a shoe box–sized parcel neatly wrapped in brown paper and tied with string. On the parcel was written, "To Dearest Connie." On the envelope, it naturally just said, "Peter." I looked around again nervously as I read the back of the envelope.

Peter. Open and read in complete private before you do anything else. Then you will know what to do, and most probably what is in the parcel. Thanks for everything. James.

The taxi ride back to Marlow was excruciating. I tried to look out of the window at the beautiful British countryside, but I couldn't stop looking at the parcel and the envelope waiting on the seat next to me. I would look up from time to time at the back of the taxi driver's head and answer some mundane question about my "shopping" trip or the weather in England compared to America, but I would quickly return my glance to the parcel and the envelope and back again.

CHAPTER 24

RED-LETTER DAY.

——

Peter. July 2009.

I CONTINUED THE DAY'S THEME of cloak-and-dagger by paying for the taxi early and walking the last few hundred yards to Forest Grange alone. To this day, I don't know why. I arrived back at the big house as everyone was sitting down in the conservatory for a cup of tea. The baby was sound asleep in Sandi's arms, and Jake asked if the pub had been busy. I hardly knew what to say, so I made some excuse and disappeared to my room.

About an hour later after reading the contents of the small dusty envelope over and over, I did indeed know exactly what to do.

James had made plans all along. He had chosen Sandi and me to tell this story; he had even included the scribbled introduction to it tucked inside the very envelope I now held. The envelope in which he entrusted the secret last chapter. Now entrusted to me.

So I gathered my thoughts, took several deep breaths, and went back downstairs.

"Um, everyone. Sorry. I have something I need to read to you all," I said probably too loudly.

"Peter! Can't it wait a bit?" Sandi hushed me. "The baby is finally asleep."

"No, well, no, I don't think it can wait. It's from Jim."

Everyone stopped what they were doing and looked up, so while I had them I continued.

"It's a letter from James. It's important."

After explaining the day's wild goose chase, I had everyone's undivided attention, and so I began to read the letter to Laura, Jake, and Connie, as sure as I could have been that it was what Jim wanted me to do.

"Dear Peter,

Thanks for being such a good friend and a great listener over the past few years. I hope what I am about to tell you won't make you think any less of me. But here goes.

You remember the boat and the old photograph and the stuff I wrote on the back of it. Well you also know that the guy kept that picture for four years without doing anything.

What I never told you was that he called me. Just after the incident on the bridge last August, he bloody well phoned me at home.

He had been drinking, I could tell from his voice. He was barely coherent, but he wanted to meet.

He said he wanted to get some stuff off his chest. I honestly thought he was going to confess something seriously interesting or useful, so I agreed to go to his house. The house you are very probably standing in right now."

That was the first time everyone realized that I was reading a letter from James about Alan Blake, and the looks began to fly as did the questions. I managed to fill in some gaps as I went, but I continued reading as best I could. James's letter from beyond the grave continued.

"So I jumped in the car and drove around the town, over the bridge, and down to Alan Blake's house as fast as I could. It must have only taken me about ten minutes. But by the time I arrived, there was no answer at the front door. It took me a while, but I made my way around the back to the garden and I looked in the conservatory windows. I banged on the glass doors, and one of them opened as I did.

So I stuck my head in and shouted, but there was no reply. I decided to go in. As I rounded the stairs and went back toward the kitchen, I could hear something. Someone was snoring. It was Blake.

He was out for the count. The stink of whiskey almost knocked me over. I slapped him a little and called out, but he was blind drunk and out cold. I slapped him again a few times, possibly for my own enjoyment, but still, I heard nothing but a faint groan.

I thought to myself, maybe it was fate? Maybe it was my chance? After all I had gone there for answers, hadn't I? But as that now looked impossible to achieve there was something else I was not leaving without. This wasn't going to be an entirely wasted trip.

Back in the grand hall, I looked up through the void beyond the incredibly high ceiling to the second-floor landing. I picked my way carefully up the huge dark-wood stairs. I came to a half landing where the staircase splits. At random, I went left and began to look for her room.

I found it eventually in the dark, dusty pigsty the house had become. I immediately located what I had come for. It was exactly where she had said it would be. I stuffed it in my jacket, zipped it up, and was off, feeling my way quietly back along the corridors and tripping over God knows what with my back to the wall.

Suddenly, the thing we all dread more than anything else happened. My bloody phone rang! It was louder than a freight train and vibrated along the oak floor after I dropped it in my panic. I got it together and pressed the red button. Then I just knelt there awhile in the dark, getting my breath back and listening for movement downstairs. All seemed quiet. Bloody hell, I thought. Onward then.

As I came to the top of the stairs, a man called out, 'Who's there?' It was Blake. He was startled, angry, and aggressive. Maybe even frightened. It dawned on me pretty quickly that even if he remembered asking me to come over, it would not look good that I had been upstairs in his house. God, I thought, what if he has a gun? All those hunting, shooting, fishing types have shotguns.

It was too late to hide. He had seen me by the time that thought crossed my mind. He shouted something like, 'Who's there?' but he was still slurring his words so much that I couldn't be sure. He was shouting who knows what louder still as he tried to get up the stairs toward me.

It all happened so fast. He was halfway up when I decided to break for it. I knew I could get past him easy enough, so I just screamed out and ran for it. I got within a few steps of him when he lost his footing on the stacks of papers. As he slid down he grabbed the side rails and his foot jammed against something which spun him up and around so his back was now turned toward me. He used his outstretched arms to stop his fall, and my path was blocked.

I know that my initial thoughts when I arrived at the house were at best to vent my anger at him, possibly if he got rough I might have wanted to do him some harm, but in my condition, I would probably have been the one to get hurt. Knowing me I am not sure I would have said or done very much if he hadn't been passed out drunk. But this was different—unplanned and almost forced upon me. Or at least it was an opportunity too good to miss.

All of my anger and hatred toward him rose with a sudden tangible burn of adrenaline, and I had my moment after all.

I gave him one big double-palmed shove in the back as I hurtled toward him. That was all it took, and like that he was flying through the air. With a sickening thud, he tumbled down and onto the marble floor. He cried out as he landed headfirst. Then silence.

I was frozen halfway down the stairs for what seemed like ages. What to do? Go. Just get out. I moved carefully past him. I wondered if I could just leave him. Should I have called the police or an ambulance? Then as I stood over him, he mumbled something, and I could hear his breathing. He was badly hurt.

The longer I stood there, the less able I was to move. I started to see him for what he was. Alan Blake. The man who had employed South. If he hadn't, Emma would still be alive today. The man whose boat my daughter was stolen away to her death in. The Alan Blake who hurt my Connie.

The hatred for him had been burning in me for years, and it was stronger than ever now as I watched him suffer.

When I arrived I wanted to have it out with him once and for all. Confront the bastard. Get him to confess to knowing South and get him to apologize for what he had done to Connie. That's why I had slipped the picture into his boat all those years ago. I wanted the confrontation. I knew about him and Steven South. He had as much to do with Emma's disappearance as South did. It's just as if Blake loaded the bullets and South fire the gun. Disgusting paedophiles like them stick together. I was going to force it out of him somehow.

Why had Blake gone to the bridge with that picture on the day of the wedding? It hadn't been to see Connie. He didn't even look at her. He had figured out who I was to Connie and he knew where we would all be on that special day. But why would he have come to the bridge and thrown the picture in the river in front of me? Any ordinary innocent man would have wanted to know what the hell I meant by it all. He knew what I was on about. He knew I was on to him.

They say a picture is worth a thousand words. Well, that picture of his boat said one word, 'Guilty.'

As I watched him I kept thinking that if only he had not associated with pedophiles like Steven South, my daughter would be with us today. I thought of poor Connie too and this bastard now lying on the marble floor in front of me, bleeding and begging for help. I liked standing there. Watching him suffer. I liked it a lot.

He pleaded with me, although his voice was weak. 'Ambulance. Doctor. Help! Help me please.' He could just about speak, but the more he did, the more blood came from his mouth. He hadn't moved an inch since he landed on the stone floor. He was trying and getting angry, but he couldn't. The more time passed, the more I realized that he couldn't move if he tried. He had broken something, probably his neck I thought and hoped. It was becoming clear to both of us that unless help came soon, Alan Blake was going to die.

So I pulled up a chair. I asked him about Emma and South and Connie, but he just smiled at me. Blood began to trickle from the corner of his mouth faster now. Good, I thought. Internal bleeding—that's good. I pulled my chair closer and leaned over him.

I stayed there for at least ten minutes and watched the fear on his face as he realized that help was not coming. He realized that he was going to die there alone, unloved, and in pain, and that I would be standing over him as he took his last breath.

I heard him take it, and I smiled. I stayed another ten minutes until I was sure. I replaced the chair, took a good look around, and left the way I had come.

I love you all. Don't judge me too harshly. I did it because I wanted to, and I enjoyed it.

The world is a better place with him gone—trust me. It might be best to keep this to ourselves, though? Burn after reading. I've always wanted to say that.

I will miss you all so very much. Love always.

James."

And with that, I looked up to see the open mouths. Before the inquisition began, I said, "There's one last thing." I produced the parcel and handed it to Connie. She cautiously untied the string and peeled off the brown paper.

Connie lovingly picked up the floppy old Dalmatian, and with tears running down her face, she said, "Dally, there you are! Thank you, James. Thank you for everything."

CHAPTER 25

WHAT THE EYE DOESN'T SEE

———

THERE WAS NATURALLY LOTS OF soul-searching once the implications of the letter had sunk in.

At that time in the life of the new Mr. and Mrs. Forester and their huge new house, they only had two staff: a newly appointed housekeeper and the original gardener. The housekeeper, a wonderful older lady named Betty Troot, couldn't do enough for Jake, Connie, and especially little Jimmy. Connie interviewed the three applicants for the position and knew right away that her new housekeeper was going to be Mrs. Troot. They got on like a house on fire, and in time Connie came to rely on her so much that a cook and a cleaner were added to the household so as to reduce Bettys' workload.

A quick nervous look around by Jake, Connie, and Laura confirmed what I already knew—which was that the gardener was clearly visible at the very bottom of the garden as he had been all day doing whatever it is gardeners do to box hedges and that Mrs. Troot had not yet returned from her twice weekly excursion to the local supermarket.

With the coast clear so to speak, Jake sat quietly, now with little baby Jimmy in his arms whilst Sandi slowly approached me and gave me a wonderful and much-needed hug. We were immediately joined by Connie and then Laura; most of us were in tears.

In whispered tones we began to talk about the obvious implications there would be should someone find out about what James had done.

Connie had after all inherited that wealth and the very house in which we were standing thanks to James and in effect what could well be interpreted by the police as murder. Jake didn't get involved one bit. In fact he was sitting happily with the baby, making funny noises much to Jimmy's amusement. I think Jake was actually proud of what his father had done. Deep down so were we all. It just took us all longer to come around to that conclusion. I think sometimes we want to accept what we feel in our hearts, but we want to know that others involved feel the same way too. We want to know that our stance on a particular issue is the same as everyone else's, and we prefer to know that before we reveal our stance.

And so it was, we all agreed very quickly that it was all good. That James had done not just us but the world a big favor. And just like that we never spoke of it again.

Mrs. Troot marched in followed by the shop boy who the supermarket supplied to carry all the bags each week, and we all melted away to our own thoughts.

The sun came flooding in, reflected off the silver river and through the huge conservatory windows. The gardener was riding the lawn mower up and down and the house was once again full of hustle and bustle and voices.

The smell of fresh bread baking in the kitchen soon filled the air and apart from the occasional knowing glance at one another, we all just put it behind us and acted as if nothing had happened. Sandi and I allowed ourselves to talk about it endlessly when we were alone, but the others never did. Jake didn't need to. He was genuinely fine with it. He missed his father, but he had his own son now and he looked after his mother and he was happy with the way it had all turned out. Connie didn't want to talk about it ever. She couldn't face up to any of it, and she certainly didn't want to have to drag up the past. But Laura? We always imagined it was hardest for her.

Laura had after all just lost her husband only then to discovered things about him which would have been hard to take. She knew she had to keep quiet for the sake of James's reputation and for Jake, Connie, and little Jimmy. Knowing how caring she is she probably even realized that Sandi and I were accessories in a way, if only after the fact. We knew enough to get in trouble should it come to that and so we all kept very quiet indeed.

Jake drove me and Sandi to the airport the following morning. We said our warmest good-byes and were well on our way back to the United States before either of us breathed. Sandi suddenly held my hand, which she usually only does if there is serious turbulence. I knew what she was thinking about; so was I.

A few weeks later in late August of 2009 I had a not unexpected phone call from Jake. We had been keeping in touch via e-mail and I was only the day before enquiring of them all. But this was not about anything remotely that mundane. I could tell from the second I heard his voice. This was serious.

A few days earlier Jake and Connie were again seated comfortably in the conservatory. Mrs. Troot was buzzing around attentively, and little baby Jimmy was asleep in his crib. All was well; the conversation was about the garden and what to do with the boathouse. What Jake meant by that was that he wanted a big new boat to go in it. He was just steering the conversation around to it when out of the corner of his eye, he saw something which halted him dead in his tracks. He literally stopped talking midway through a sentence, froze for a second before jumping to his feet and rushing across the open room to the foot of the stairs. Connie was naturally asking him what was wrong, and as she did so, she looked at what Jake was now pointing to as he said, "What the fuck is that?" Then in a flash she was standing with him, and they both knew exactly what it was. It was a very small, very discreetly positioned security camera.

No one had noticed it before. It was installed in the woodwork of a picture frame and pointing out across the foot of the stairs.

No one knew if it was real or live or how long it had been there.

Jake got a ladder from the garage and quickly covered the camera lens with sticky tape. Then he traced the wire from the back of the picture frame, along a wooden rail and through the wall to a hallway behind the huge staircase. From there the wire ran the length of the hall behind another decorative wooden rail and out into the office. It was connected to a wireless Internet router, and the power light was on.

Jake switched it off and ran back to Connie who was now standing holding Jimmy while she looked up at the camera and down at the foot of the stairs.

Neither of them knew what to do. Who put the camera there? When did they put it there? Why? And most importantly, where was the footage stored?

It took Jake about forty-eight very sleepless hours to find the paperwork in a mountain of old files belonging to Alan Blake. The camera was the only one remaining of the three fitted in April of 2001 by a firm called M and F Alarm Systems of High Wycombe.

Jake and Connie discussed what to do. If the system was even still working, who was to say that it was on or triggered or recording on that night. And if it was, it would probably be automatically wiped off by now. Jake seemed convinced that any footage would only be viewed if it was requested by the house owner, and if it wasn't requested after a few weeks, then the hard drive it was on would record the next footage in its place. Connie reminded Jake of the time I had stood at the foot of the stairs and read the letter out loud, and Jake realized that it was only a few weeks ago and he was immediately more worried.

They couldn't decide whether to call the alarm people. Doing nothing would mean in time the evidence, if it existed, would inevitably be recorded over or destroyed. Calling them could alert them to the footage unnecessarily.

Connie called them the next day.

A lovely, helpful chap named Mr. Muhar Ifran answered the phone. He had been the owner of M and F Alarms since its inception ten years earlier. It was soon clear he knew all there was to know about alarm systems and security cameras. He also knew all about the sudden demise of Mr. Blake. Connie was able to introduce herself as Blake's daughter and receive condolences and then the relevant information.

Mr. Ifran was sorry to hear about her tragic loss. He was also mortified to find out that she had inherited the house. Not because he didn't like Connie but because he had unwittingly thought the house was still empty, and as such, he had long since given up the bad debt, cancelled the contract, and switched everything off at his end. He did offer to reinstate everything and was even cheeky enough to ask if Connie was calling to pay the outstanding invoices. Connie was quick to assure him that he would be paid and that for now at least, she was not in the market for a security system. Jake had in fact only just appointed a firm that would eventually install a new state-of-the-art alarm system, but there was no need to hurt the man's feelings by telling him that, so she didn't.

While Connie had the nice Pakistani man's attention and Jake leant in to hear the phone conversation, she inquired when the system was shut down, to which Mr. Ifran said that he had switched it off and closed the account about three weeks after Mr. Blake died. He also recalled that it must have been shortly after that on September 23, 2008, when—and Mr. Muhar Ifran was sure of the date because it was the day of his eldest daughter's birthday—a police officer came for the camera footage.

Connie almost collapsed. Jake steadied her by the arm, but even he was struggling to keep it together. She made her excuses and politely hung up. They had both clearly heard what he'd said.

The game was up.

Jake and Connie knew they were in big trouble now. Then as they dissected the information, they realized that the footage from the day of Alan Blake's death may or may not be on the hard drive, and even if it was, it only incriminated James. There was no footage from when I had read to them James's letter because that was almost a year later, and as such, no one would ever know that they had, in some small way, covered the whole thing up. Jake reminded Connie that a lot of time had passed, the estate had been settled, and that if anything had been on the hard drive, the police would have been involved before now. It had been nearly a year since Blake's death, and if the police had anything on James, they would have revealed it by now.

I concurred with Jake. Alan Blake had died in September of 2008. If the police had anything, we would know by now surely, and after a few reassuring words to Connie, I hung up and went home to tell Sandi.

———

Time past and we kept in touch as we always did. Nothing had ever come of the camera thing and life was settling down nicely. In fact almost another full year had gone by and it was the June of 2010 when Sandi the girls and I were invited to spend a week with all our English friends at 'Forest Grange'.

Connie Jake and Laura wanted to get everyone together to remember James a year on from his passing and "much more importantly" Laura said, to celebrate the first birthday of little Jimmy.

There were lots of people there, most of which I did not recognize. Some new friends of Jakes and some old faces I only knew the names of from James' story.

We had a few nice days together all of us at the big house and I even got to drive Jakes fancy new boat. We took it down to Marlow and back sharing the driving and a few beers much as his father and I had done before.

On Saturday afternoon the house filled up again and the wine flowed. The guests were largely inside admiring the work which had been done to the place whilst I was standing alone at the water's edge looking out across at the opposite river bank to the spot where James stopped his boat that day.

"I thought I would find you here Peter" Jake said.

And I turned to see Jake approaching me with another man.

Before any introductions could take place the stranger simply thrust out a small black plastic box and said, "Jake wanted me to give this to you, I suspect James would have wanted it too" and as the man looked at Jake he said to us, "my guess is you boys will know exactly what to do with it"

I took the hard drive and stared at it for a while. I suspected what it was before I saw the bright blue sticker on its underside which read; "Property of M and F alarms."

The man introduced himself as Mark Benson and he told me that the nice Mr. Ifran had handed over the security footage hard drive without looking too closely at the expired police identification.

Mark went on to explain why he acted on such a hunch and that he alone had watched the footage in all its clarity. It turned out that he had spent the past year of his retirement investigating the former owner of this illustrious house and discovering the link between Blake, South, Connie and therefore James. Mark naturally developed a great sympathy for James and his family following the disappearance of their daughter Emma some Twenty Five years ago. He had grown to know and like the Forester family over that period of his career and it was a huge personal regret that he hadn't managed to solve the case. He pieced it all together as any good investigating officer would do and had a pretty good idea of what had transpired on the grand stair case that fateful night. Whatever his true motivation was Mark had decided that this sleeping dog would be best left lying where it was.

So there I stood on the river bank with Jake and former inspector Benson, holding the little black box in my hand, knowing what we all wanted to do with it. I gestured with my eyes, took their nod of approval, swiveled on my heels and threw the hard drive into the center of the fast flowing river.

The end.

ABOUT THE AUTHOR.

Stuart Maskell was born in Henley-on-Thames, England, in June of 1969 and has lived most of his life in the small beachside village of Croyde-Bay in Devon, England.

Maskell is a successful house builder developer and author. Happily married with two wonderful children, Maskell enjoys traveling and spending as much time as possible with his family and their dog 'Jimmy' at their home in the French Alps.

Other work by Stuart Maskell now available;

"DUE."

When accountant Anthony Pride, the fall guy for his gangster bosses is sent down for ten years, his beautiful and vulnerable young wife Kat must fend for herself in what rapidly becomes a dangerous world. Preyed upon by the very men responsible for the couple's predicament she discovers a hidden propensity for extreme violence in order to clear a path for Anthony's release and free herself from the unwanted advances of the Nastasi crime family. This unsuspecting femme fatale must execute her elaborate and brutal plan then hide in plain sight, open a secret channel of communication with her incarcerated husband and above all make sure everyone gets what they are DUE.

And soon to be available;

————

"The Eyes Have It".
A controversial and cautionary tale of the western political
system and its vulnerability to a "hostile" take
over through its very own 'democratic' electoral
system.
Set in and around Westminster 2055 as the M.P's
from one relatively new party begin to exercise their
majority in the house, their power over the law of the
land and its unsuspecting populous.

————

"Till Death Do Us Start".
The graphic tale of a serial killer's life told in reverse.
From the last murder to the first and the changes he
goes through to arrive back at normality.

————

"Jeff, Sue, Bob"
The very quirky tale of a seemingly ordinary, elderly,
married couple
and the other man in 'both' their lives!

————

I sincerely hope you enjoyed this book.
I am working hard on the next for you so please stay
tuned for more information.

————

You can find
more about me and my other titles at;
www.stumaskell.wix.com/stumaskell
You can also follow me at;
www.facebook.com/stuart.maskell1
Twitter; @stumaskell
#thegirlwiththethousandyardstare

Printed in Great Britain
by Amazon